HAPPINESS
AND OTHER FICTIONS

HERSH DOVID NOMBERG (1876–1927) was born in Mszczonow (Yiddish: Ashminov) a market town about thirty miles from Warsaw. Orphaned at a young age, he was raised by his maternal grandfather in a devoutly religious milieu. He began publishing poems and short stories around 1900 in both Yiddish and Hebrew and was considered one of the most influential Yiddish writers of his generation. Nomberg died at the age of 51, having suffered from chronic lung problems for most of his life.

DANIEL KENNEDY is a translator and editor based in France. Among his translations are Zalman Shneour's *A Death: Notes of a Suicide* (Wakefield Press, 2019) and Hersh Dovid Nomberg's *A Cheerful Soul and Other Stories* (Snuggly Books, 2021).

SNUGGLY BOOKS

HERSH DOVID NOMBERG

HAPPINESS
AND OTHER FICTIONS

TRANSLATED BY
DANIEL KENNEDY

THIS IS A SNUGGLY BOOK

ISBN: 978-1-64525-101-9

CONTENTS

HAPPINESS
AND OTHER FICTIONS

SUMMER HOME

The lamp has gone out.

I'm lying alone in the room, eyes open, surveying the darkness around me. I can't get to sleep.

A long chain of thoughts stretches out before me, slow and oppressive.

Just before the flame went out, it flickered. It sprang into the air; trying with all its might to burn, it flared up. In the end it spluttered and died, leaving nothing behind but a bad smell.

Why didn't I just put out the lamp? I ask myself. Wasn't it for the fresh air that I came to this summer home in the first place?

What is this wicked inclination that compels me? I enjoyed watching the thing struggle in vain, giving everything it had and tiring itself out, clasping impotently to life when there was hope. It inspired a feeling of mockery in my heart, a feeling I love passionately.

It reminded me of how, as a child, I would stand callously at the bed of a dying man, scrutinizing his face, until his soul left his body. And the weeping of those present would only encourage me . . .

I recall now so clearly the death of my teacher Reb Mendl: I thought I could hear the rasping from his gullet, and see his face, moving in spasms . . . I imagine that by now his face has lost all its hair, all its skin . . . Bony skulls like that can fetch a good price, back there in the big city that I've left behind.

In the darkness I touch my head: it still has hair and skin. And who is the person who will stand at my bedside when I die, and passionately observe my face as it moves with spasms?

And who is the person who will find *my* bony head, and sell it, later using the money to satisfy their every heart's desire?

※

O, heavy mood of mine! Where to escape from you? When one's lungs are ailing, one comes to stay at a summer home, to breathe the fresh air—but if one's soul is sick, where does one go?

Outside is as quiet as death.

Just now a dog barked.

I'm thankful for the noise; the voice of a living creature is comforting, even that of a dog.

An echo answers from the small wood nearby. A short pause. The dog barks once again, the echo responds.

And to the dog it seems as though one of his own kind is calling out to him from the trees, and he continues to bark, louder and louder each time . . . Just now I heard the patter of his paws; he's run up to the fence and is barking in anger. The echo responds.

The dog is agitated now. If he could only catch that

other one, he would surely sink his teeth into him with such fury; he paces back and forth, driven mad with rage. The echo responds.

What will happen in the end?

It goes on like this for a long, long time.

My eyes grow heavy. I feel sleep begin to overpower me.

A fog settles down inside my head, making itself at home—Ach! begone profane thoughts! Let a weary man get some rest!

But one thought in particular creeps slowly into my mind: are we any cleverer than that dog out there?

What is our existence exactly? What are our deeds, all our rushing about in life? Are we not calling out to our own echos? Are we not chasing our own shadows? Are we not frightened by the reflection of our own faces?

I want to open my eyes, but I cannot. A sign, I think, that I am very close to sleep. But I can still hear the dog barking, and the echo's response. Both voices are close now, right here next to my bed.

And once again, a thought creeps in:

When the dog dies, a new one will take its place, and the barking will continue, and the echo will respond, making this new dog agitated and angry and he too will run around as if crazy.

My arms and legs feel welded down, I want to move, but I cannot. Oh, how tired I am. Sleep comes soon.

And the dog barks and barks; the echo responds.

I will just fall asleep, and will not wait for the end.

1907

RAYA-MANO

I

The Land of the Five Rivers, where the sun blazes so hot overhead and the lotus flower blooms, was blessed with prophets who had been gifted to the people to teach them and to be their helpers and guides along the thorny path of life, and beyond, through the somber gates of death. The words of the prophets filled the people's hearts with solace; their names rang out throughout the land, and a common blessing for every mother was: "May God grant you a prophet from your loins."

The people of that land—in particular those tribes that dwelled along the banks of the holy Ganges—did not forget their ancient lineage; amid the chaos of life, they passed it on from father to child, from one generation to the next. The old legends told of a noble, highborn race, descended from the gods themselves, who were sent down to the pitiable earth to atone for their sins. For that reason their souls forever resounded with a tone of mourning, and their hearts remained open and attentive towards the spirit and matters of the intellect.

They held work in low regard, and mere subsistence was not enough to give their lives meaning; they loved to be idle, to do nothing, to think and dream; they would lie for hours on the grass, engaged in longing introspection of the profundity of the heavens and the abyss of their own souls. Opium—that intoxicating substance, weaver of enchanted and alluring fantasies—had yet to be discovered in those days, and so people turned instead to the living word, direct from the mouths of the prophets, which enlivened and ennobled them.

There were two kinds of prophets, prophets of Sorrow and prophets of Mirth, and both preached the same message:

"The world is a great conflagration. Every desire in one's heart is a piece of straw cast into the flames; every want, a fiery new tongue that devours. For want breeds want and desire breeds desire, and so the fire is vast and eternal. Why toil to fulfil one's heart's desires when the heart can never be appeased, and the spirit can never be sated? The will to live is but a tiny spark in one's heart: blow upon it, and behold! It ignites, and you stand amid the flames and you did not bring any water to put them out, you added nothing but kindling and wood."

These were the teachings of the prophets, and the people listened and took their words to heart.

When a prophet of Sorrow spoke his voice quivered softly; rich in mercy, it floated, and, like the tones of a distant harp swimming through the dark night, it seeped into the people's hearts, soothing and restoring them. People listened with their hearts, ruminating on their destiny, and on their ceaseless toil.

And when the prophet of Mirth spoke his voice was limpid and pure, as pure as the voice of a silver bell. He did not chastise, preferring to ridicule the world and its sinful follies. He unraveled—thread by thread—the great web that fantasy had woven around the human spirit in order to entangle and ensnare it with multiplicity, toil and worry. The people heard his words, and they were refreshed and enlivened by them.

Each prophet was elected to his holy calling while still in his mother's belly, the good news being revealed to the mother as soon as she was with child. When the infant emerged from his mother's womb, he would stand straight up on his feet, take seven steps forward and bow before the gathered crowd. And they would behold: if a furrow appeared on his brow, it was a sign he would grow up to be a prophet of Sorrow; but if a smile appeared on his lips, then they knew that he was destined to be a prophet of Mirth.

By the banks of the holy Ganges, there stood, in those days, an old building which housed the temples of the god of Sorrow and the god of Mirth. The entrance to the temple of Sorrow was over dry land. Whoever had cleansed his soul and his body according to the rituals was led inside by the priests, who removed the veil from the holy idol, revealing a sorrowful face—eyes full of grief, and a forehead darkened by a heavy cloud of purest hardship. The entrance to the temple of Mirth, on the other hand, was reached by passing over the water. One first had to board a small boat, alone, and navigate the hasty currents which raged in that place. One needed to show contempt for death, and upon safely making it through, one had the honor of beholding the holy likeness of the god of Mirth, with his deep, kindly eyes, the laugh-lines on either side of his mouth, and the many wrinkles on his brow, which told of sadness gone by, of life and its troubles vanquished, of mountains levelled, and of the abyss filled with the ash of a heart that had consumed itself.

When he came of age, the prophet of Sorrow's path led him straight to his god, while a prophet of Mirth had to endure the arduous journey before he could be deemed holy enough to stand before his god.

But woe be to the prophet of Mirth who even once in his life caught a glimpse of the god of Sorrow, and woe be to the prophet of Sorrow for whom the face of the other god was uncovered. For this was considered a grave transgression against their respective spirits, a sin which could never be washed away. They were doomed to wander the earth, exiled and cursed wherever they went.

This was known by all.

II

And when Raya-Mano's mother, a pious woman, rich in virtue, became pregnant with him, a godly man came to import to her the news that she carried a prophet inside her belly.

And the godly man said: "I see a small cloud rising in your clear sky, and I see a black stain tarnishing your happiness, O pious woman rich in virtue—but I know not how to interpret these signs."

And she bore a son, and the infant immediately walked seven paces forward, and two paces back and bowed, whereupon a wrinkle appeared on his brow. Everyone then knew that a prophet of Sorrow had been born.

But to everyone's surprise a tiny, barely discernible smile appeared on the child's lips.

And when the child was weaned, his mother brought him before the idol of Sorrow, where she made the appropriate offerings according to the rituals, and so the young Raya-Mano was raised by the prophets and priests to be a prophet of Sorrow.

In time, however, they perceived strange omens pertaining to the child. On occasion he would kneel before the holy image of his god, his eyes open to absorb the sadness that poured forth from the idol's eyes, and a holiness would settle upon the child's face. But then suddenly his lips would tremble and something akin to the hint of a smile passed over them.

This was without precedent, and the holy books had nothing to advise on the matter.

They sent for his mother and they asked her: "O pious woman rich in virtue, you mother of a prophet! Tell us! Did you not visit the temple of Mirth, the one on this side of the river? Because we do not know what is wrong with your son, or whether he will bring great joy or great unhappiness to the children of the earth."

"No, I did not set foot in the temple of the god, but a holy man brought me the news that I would bear a prophet, and he said: "I see a black stain tarnishing your happiness."

The priests listened, shook their heads, and looked on the growing prophet with great trepidation.

They did not let him go outside, and they told everyone who spoke to the child not to utter the name of the god of Mirth in his presence, and that he must never learn of the godly idol that stood with its face turned toward the crashing waves.

And so the child was raised, secluded and hidden from the world, alone with the holy books. His heart grew with the suffering of all worlds, with the great sadness that dwells within the living and the dead, and his voice grew purer with each passing day; it poured trembling like the tones of a harp, swimming through the dark night from some unseen place in the distance.

But the young prophet did not find peace. He sank deeper into his contemplations and, in doing so, was overcome by the great sorrow of the world, whereupon his soul poured forth soft, pale sounds, and the Divine Presence of sorrow settled upon him, shining down from his pure countenance. But his heart was struck by an unfamiliar reverberation, beset by a distant vision of laughing eyes, a mocking face and a strange, unfamiliar world. Where had he seen those eyes before? When had he lived in that other world? What was the meaning of the gnawing in his heart? And where did he come from? What was he doing there and what did he seek?

These thoughts lasted no more than a moment, but for many days and weeks his heart did not know rest.

Sometimes his sleep was interrupted by a sudden terrible fear; his heart raced. The god of Mirth appeared to him in his dreams; his face frightened him, and yet his heart was drawn toward him, and his soul yearned for him.

Then one night, waking in a terrible fright, he roused the oldest of the priests and poured out his heart for him:

"I fell asleep while I was contemplating the great Sorrow," he told him. "But in my dream an old gray man revealed himself to me. He was calm, smirking and full of laughter, and he stared at me with those eyes of his . . ."

"What sort of eyes were they?" Asked the old servant of god.

"Kindly, deep and full of peace and sympathy . . . yet mockery, such great mockery lay in them too . . . and on his lips—laughter . . . the kind of laughter that cuts right through a person . . . I am frightened, holy man! A wicked spirit plagues me, help me, holy man."

The old man rose from his bed in the middle of the night, and led the boy toward the fire he had lit. By the light of the fire he studied the boy's face until he discerned two small lines on either side of the boy's mouth.

"Terrible!" the old man thought in his heart, but to the boy he said nothing; he neither consoled him, nor attempted to dampen his fear.

III

One day, alone within the four empty walls of the temple, Raya-Mano strained his ears to hear the roar of the waves crashing outside. It seemed to him that something important was happening beyond the walls; boats were coming and going and he imagined he could hear the splash of paddles and the footsteps of many people jumping ashore onto hard marble stone. His old teacher was troubled that day and he watched the boy with mounting disquiet.

"Something is going to happen today," Raya-Mano thought, but he did not say anything to the old man, nor did he ask him anything. From that night onward they began to grow distant from each other. The young prophet no longer said what was on his mind, and the old man no longer confided in him as before; the old man no longer kissed him, nor patted the boy's head with his old, trembling hands, and today they stood further apart and more isolated from one another than ever before.

And at night Raya-Mano wandered in his sleep; he strained his ear to discern every movement, every sound from outside. Throughout the long years spent alone within those four walls, with only his own spirit and the holy books for companionship, he had honed his hearing so that now, despite the strength and thickness of the walls, his ears were sharp enough to pick up the tiniest echo from afar. He had an inkling that the crowds outside were gathered for an important ceremony to honor the god who was unknown to him. By midnight the noise died down and Raya-Mano could all but picture the masses dropping to their knees in silent prayer. After a moment of stillness, the air began to tremble with the sound of holy chants. Once a year a similar rite was performed there for the god of Sorrow, where the people also kneeled until midnight, whereupon the silence gave way to song. But the chanting he heard now was different. It stemmed from a different source and flowed toward a different sea. It was not a song whose plaintive tones, rigid and stiff, seemed frozen within its own borders. These melodies gamboled and chased one another, tangling and untangling themselves in a merry dance; in them the stars winked at each other, and the sun laughed at the moon.

The young prophet pressed his ear to the wall, and his spirit thirstily drank in the new songs. A kind of intoxication gripped him, chasing away the great sorrow, and seeping into his spirit, into every chamber of his soul, tearing down its walls and infecting it. But how sweet was the poison! It brought with it echoes of a new world and for all the destruction it wrought, it also brought a feeling of comfort and cleansing. Raya-Mano stood there listening all night long.

Then, just before dawn, as the eastern sky began to turn pale, the chanting stopped and a heavy silence blanketed everything around. The boy was frightened; he had been left alone with his desolated, ruined soul, and he began to weep in terrible pain, tearing out his beautiful locks with his hands.

"What is wrong with you?" the old man asked in alarm.

"I listened, I heard . . ." the boy stammered. "The whole night long. There was a ceremony outside, a holy day for a god I do not know . . . my heart has been laid waste, my soul is destroyed. Tell me, old man, tell me what does it mean, what did I hear? For my fear is so great, I'm sure it will kill me."

"What exactly did you hear?" the old man asked.

"I heard chanting, holy songs to a strange god . . ."

"What sort of chanting?

"Chants of laughter, of mockery; they frolicked, entangled themselves in a wild dance, and they penetrated deep into my soul in order to destroy it and to build it anew. And I listened, I listened the whole night and their magic held me captive. I could picture large flocks of white doves, and throngs of black crows flying, circling overhead, all night, until sunrise . . . Now I am alone, desolate. Don't leave me, my father!"

But the old man did not respond. He did not console the boy, and did not speak to his heart to appease his fear. He remained silent and shook his gray head.

Rayo-Mano fell at the old man's feet, kissing the dust before him, weeping and begging:

"Do not leave me, old man. Behold, my young heart cannot bear the great burden of longing. Look, the fear devours a new piece of me with each passing day, and you have withheld your consolation, it has been weeks since your dry lips have kissed me, and your thin fingers have long stopped stroking the hair on my head. My pain is great, and I see no way out. It's another world out there, different songs. Why do you hide the new world from me? What secret are you hiding from me in your heart, old man? Help me, holy father, help me!"

The old man listened in silence. Pressing his hands on his breast, he said:

"There is nothing I can say to you, my child. A terrible danger hangs over your young head, and there is nothing I can do to help."

IV

The time came when Raya-Mano could no longer restrain his yearning heart. One night he quietly left the four walls and stole away, hiding himself like a thief or a criminal. He filled his lungs with fresh air, and gazed up at the deep blue of the sky, at the masses of stars, large and small, and at the foggy stains of the Milky Way above. He saw them, but his spirit was unable to take them in and they did not become part of the fabric of his soul. Ever since the worm of doubt had begun gnawing into his heart the whole world had begun to feel alien, unfamiliar, and disconnected. He walked all night, back and forth, along the banks of the holy Ganges, and by the first rays of daylight he saw the temple whose gates opened out into the water, and he understood that here was the house of that strange god.

The following night he made his way by boat across the tumultuous currents and arrived safely at the gate. With a trembling hand, he removed the veil from the holy idol, and the god of Mirth was revealed before his eyes. It stood there, unmoving, and regarded the child with its laughing eyes. The young prophet was instantly charmed, and fell to his knees, hugging the feet of the holy god. This is what he had been seeking for so long: the figure that had revealed itself to him in a dream! And like one who has had a membrane removed from his eyes to see the world in all its brightness, so Raya-Mano saw a new brilliance and a new world. In that holy face, in the wrinkles of its brow, all the sufferings of the world had been collected; the great sorrow dwelled within them, but it had been transformed into laughter. The pain of the world laughed out from behind those eyes, all that terrible pain and sorrow. The whole world with its web of multiplicity had been transformed into laughter. Raya-Mano stood there all night, greedily drinking in the laughter that poured from the godly eyes, and the boy's heart was transformed.

He came every night, alone, to serve his new god, to drink from its deep spring, and the thirst of his spirit was never quenched.

One night, however, a curious thing happened:

Raya-Mano was kneeling before his god with praise and song, bound to it with body and soul, drawn towards it as iron is drawn to a magnet, but as he kissed the holy idol, spreading his arms around it, he felt that the image on the other side of the idol was the same. He walked around it slowly and came to a halt—there he saw the familiar figure of the god of Sorrow. It was terrible to behold: it was one body with two faces, and the two faces were the same: one single figure, but the face on one side was laughing, while that on the other side was mourning. Raya-Mano saw what no prophet or holy man had ever seen before him: he beheld the two-fold spirit, the two-fold form: Mirth and Sorrow, flowing from the wellspring of one and the same god.

From that moment on Raya-Mano wandered the earth, and his spirit no longer knew peace.

He was a prophet, and as a prophet he had been sanctified in his mother's belly, but the people did not know him, did not honor him and could not draw solace from his spirit.

Raya-Mano would preach before the crowds. His face beamed and his dexterous tongue made a mockery of the suffering and toil of the people and the gods throughout time; his voice resounded like the ringing of a silver bell, and pain turned to laughter, suffering to mirth. But then suddenly, the crowd would hear an echo of great sorrow, as his soul burst, pouring out soft words of longing . . . the people heard this, but did not know what it meant.

At other times, as he reproached the crowds—rousing their hearts, lamenting the torment of mankind and of all living creatures, his voice trembling, floating in the air like the plucking of a far away harp, great sorrow pouring forth from his spirit. But suddenly his spirit would transform, the expression on his face would change, and in such moments his lamentations were drowned out by the sound of laughter . . . Upon hearing this the people became furious that the beautiful melody had been interrupted; they expressed this anger toward the prophet who could do nothing but divide people's minds.

"That is no prophet, but a madman," the people cried.

24

And when he raised his voice to speak, the children mocked him and pelted him with filth.

And so the prophet fled the inhabited regions and went to live with the ascetics in the desert, where, like them, he punished and purified his body, staring directly at the sun for days on end, so that his eyes would hurt, learning to withstand all pain silently and patiently, as the ascetics teach. But he did not become a holy man. He was suddenly overcome by the spirit of Mirth, and looking into the sun, his sore eyes laughed at the pain, making a mockery of the world and of the teachings of asceticism.

And so Raya-Mano approached the prophets of Mirth, to no avail. For in the midst of a fit of laughter he was overcome by the spirit of Sorrow, and his voice began to tremble and yearn.

Thus Raya-Mano lived out his years, isolated, without friends or lovers, alone and abandoned, hounded and harassed by the youths in the streets.

He had seen the two-fold figure, and was forever punished for his sin.

And when he died no one lamented his passing; he was not buried alongside the prophets, and his name was not remembered fondly. But there was one man who lived then in those lands, a wise man who had traveled through many countries and had seen many peoples and had collected knowledge from many places, and he said:

"Honor the name of Raya-Mano. He bore the greatest suffering of the spirit."

1909

SHEKER AND SHLIMAZL

I
Loyal Friendship

The two heroes of this story still live in this world, and so to avoid any complaints I shall forgo calling them by their real names, instead referring to one as "Sheker" and the other as "Shlimazl". By the same token I shall refrain from describing their physical appearance—it will suffice for you to know that both were pale; both had eyes red from long sleepless nights, with dark blue patches under those eyes; both had reddish noses; both wore crumpled hats; their trousers and coats were either too long or too loose, too tight or too short; and they both enjoyed a daily stroll in the Saxon Garden.

They had grown up in small towns, surrounded by fields and plum-orchards, and had cultivated a love of nature. Mother nature on the other hand—cruel, capricious, mistress that she is—did not reciprocate their devotion; she drove them from their homes, separated them from their parents, robbed them of their sincere faith and piety, and chased them as far as the big city, to Warsaw, to seek out new faith, new beliefs and an occupation, relegating them for the time being—a matter of five years already—to out of the way corners: Sheker—now a property clerk—she placed high up on the fourth floor of a building on Smocza Street, while Shlimazl, now a Hebrew teacher, she pocketed in a dark third-floor attic-room on Franciszkańska Street.

It will therefore come as no surprise that their hearts drew them toward the Saxon Garden to breathe in the fresh air—they both suffered from chronic coughs—to feast their eyes on the green leaves of the trees, the fresh grass, and the flowers, and indeed to catch a glimpse through half-squinting eyes—they were both short-sighted—at the lovely, world-famous Warsaw ladies and pass comment on their relative charms and elegance. What better place was there than the Saxon Garden to engage in debates? They would argue about various topics—they were both quite erudite—such as collectivism vs. individualism; realism vs. symbolism; beauty, et cetera—in short about the enduring un-derpinnings of the universe, those crowning lights of human life.

A summer's day. Five in the evening. Warsaw is abustle; carriages clatter across the cobblestones, trams ring their bells and the worn-out, sweaty masses rush around like madmen. The air is thick. Franciszkańska Street is dominated by the stench of the leatherworks—it's enough to choke on; while Smocza Street stinks of nothing in particular, save for its habitual cocktail of unpleasant odors. Smoke from the factories blows in from the direction of Wola, the sky is black . . . What a delight, then, on days such as these, to remember the Saxon Garden, with its seven gates, open to the world in every direction, with its high trees and green leaves, it's fresh grass and cool air.

Sheker and Shlimazl did indeed follow their hearts' desire and headed to the garden, strolling down the tree-lined promenades, exploring each meandering pathway; sitting to rest on a bench, passing the time in conversation.

Sometimes they denigrated one another, and Sheker would say to Shlimazl:

"Tell me, Shlimazl, what will ever become of you?"

"And what will become of you, Sheker? Five years you've been in Warsaw already and haven't achieved a thing. A disgrace, it's beneath your dignity to languish—"

"*You*'re lecturing *me*, Shlimazl? And what do you do that's so important? You scrape together three rubles a month giving Hebrew lessons. You call that a living?"

Shlimazl thought for a moment and said:

"You understand my predicament then; my problem is that I can't afford to dress well. If I could dress the part I could earn six rubles a month, maybe even ten. But that's easier said than done. It's a vicious circle: no money, no smart clothes; no smart clothes, no money. But I have not given up hope; I'll figure something out. One way or another I'll find a way. You, on the other hand, wallow in the mud, that's it— 'Not your problem' you say . . ."

"Since when have you been so pessimistic, Shlimazl? We're both trapped in the same vicious circle. If I were well dressed I'd get a promotion, earning forty, maybe fifty rubles a month. We'd live, like kings, like God in France! But what's the use of all this talk? There's no cash, brother, and breaking our heads worrying about it is not going to change anything. Your belly is full, you're sitting here in the Saxon Garden and the sun is shining. What more could you want, fool that you are? This is the life! "

"It's an empty life," Shlimazl sighed.

"*Ozer dalim hoshiom no*," Sheker sang under his breath.

"Go to hell!" muttered Shlimazl angrily.

"Why don't *you* go to hell!"

"You turn my stomach like bitter horseradish."

"And you disgust me like bitter horseradish with candy-sugar on top," joked Sheker.

"I can't bear to look at your ugly mug."

"And you think your mug is any easier to stomach?"

This is how Sheker and Shlimazl would argue, though naturally they would soon make up, and resume walking together every day—whether it was a weekday, a holiday, or the Sabbath—without fail.

One day Sheker the property clerk walked down the promenade where he usually met his friend. He walked the length of the promenade a second time, and a third, but there was no sign of Shlimazl the Hebrew teacher. He went to investigate the other paths, turning now right, now left, keeping one myopic eye out for a crumpled hat in the distance. He strode with great haste, looking each person in the eye as he passed, before eventually admitting defeat. He sat down on a bench to wait. He waited in vain. Shlimazl was nowhere to be found.

"Where is Shlimazl?" thought Sheker, "Where can that madman have gotten to?"

But the "madman" did not turn up the following day either, nor the one after.

Sheker grew bored; the Saxon Garden lost its appeal for him. Nothing to do, no one to talk to. Solitude.

"It's a wonder," thought Sheker to himself, slouching on the bench. "You know someone for so long and don't even know where he lives, or where to find him! If only I knew his Jewish name, I'd be able to look him up at the Address Bureau. Who knows how many families with the surname Shlimazl there are in this great abyss called Warsaw?"

In the end he did go to the Address Bureau. They handed him a piece of paper with the addresses of several Shlimazls, but only one of them was a twenty-seven year old: Nosn-Note Shlimazl of number ** Smocza street. Sheker surmised that this must be his friend, Shlimazl.

He went to the address but there was no one at home. However, on the following day he rose early to try again and at nine in the morning the two friends were reunited, finding themselves together in Shlimazl's room. Shlimazl lay on his bed with a coat over him; his feet, uncovered up to the ankles, poked out from underneath. His hair was disheveled and he looked terribly melancholic. A palpable resentment filled his heart.

"Damn it, man!" said Sheker to cheer him up, "Where have you been all this time? I was half expecting to find you here hanging from a rope, or lying poisoned in your own bed!"

"If only it were so," mumbled Shlimazl.

"Come now, you ninny, don't just scowl at me like that. Tell me what happened!"

"What happened? Nothing happened: they wouldn't let me into the Saxon Garden."

"What do you mean they wouldn't let you in? Who wouldn't let you in, and why not?"

"Why not? No reason why not, the guard didn't like the look of my hat, that's all."

"Aha . . . so that's the story!"

"It's simple really. I approach, and the guard who sat watching the gates gives me a good looking over, from head to toe, and blocks my way. '*Von,* away with you!' he says, but I don't want to go, so I start arguing with him: '*Kak, shto*? I'm an intellectual, I'm a teacher, what's the meaning of not letting me in?' He looks at me again with his insolent eyes and says, 'Your hat is not in order, *barin*, and look at the state of your jacket!' And to top it all off he had the nerve to address me with informal pronouns, what insolence!"

"So?"

"So I tried to get in by force, and they brought me to the police station."

"And?"

"And? That's not enough for you? That's nothing, is it? At the police station they gave me a good beating. Maybe you, Sheker, would let them spit in your face, but if one loses all self-respect, then one is no better than a beast!"

"There's no need to get angry, why are you taking it out on me? Go on then, let it out!"

"What am I, an outcast from human society? A beggar? Do I not toil as hard as the next man?"

"Nevermind all that, of course you're not an outcast from human society, but between you and me, 'toil' isn't exactly the word I'd use in your case. But enough idle words. What have we got to be ashamed of, Shlimazl? After all, we've both got our strength, and you can't say that our lives are so bitterly hard."

"Why did you come?" said Shlimazl, starting to lose his temper, "Who asked you to call on me? Sticking your nose into another man's business . . ."

Now Sheker too felt offended. His red eyes were on the verge of tears. He straightened his hat, to signal that he intended to leave. But Shlimazl, it seemed, did not want him to leave and proceeded to change his tone.

"Can you imagine what an insult it was, what a humiliation! My God, I'm a human being after all, with thoughts and feelings, and they threw me out like a dog! I have no right to walk in the same park as all those upstanding gentlemen; my proximity alone would sully them, without me even having to touch them? I wept with shame, wept like a child."

Sheker's hat sat aslant once again, a sign that he intended to stay after all. He sat down on the bed next to his friend, and took his measure with a loving, tender gaze.

"You know, Shlimazl, it just wasn't the same without you. I couldn't find you anywhere, and I missed you somehow."

"Really?" Shlimazl asked, half sitting up in bed, his emaciated, sunken chest peeking out from under his grubby shirt.

"Look how skinny you are, Shlimazl!" said Sheker, "All skin and bone!"

"You're hardly a heavy-weight champion yourself."

"How's your cough?"

"Still there, and yours?"

"Could be worse."

Shlimazl was sitting up straight now. Sheker slid closer to him.

"It's good to have at least one close friend," said Sheker. "While I was missing you, I at least felt some connection to another living being."

"What do you mean, Sheker?"

"Listen, Shlimazl, let's be good friends, what use is all this business, give me your paw!"

With girlish bashfulness, Shlimazl gave him his hand. Sheker moved his pale face closer to Shimazl's equally pale face. Two red noses, and two pairs of red eyes, surrounded by pale rings came together. And they kissed.

So it was that Sheker and Shlimazl sealed the pact of friendship and are as devoted to each other to this day as a bride and groom, as a young couple, budding with happiness, beaming with pleasure in each other's companionship.

II
A Game for Three

Toward the north of Warsaw, not far beyond the bustling courtyards of Nalewki Street, meadows stretch out as far as the eye can see. This is the Citadel district where the city comes to an abrupt, almost violent end, and the high multi-story buildings look straight down over unbuilt, uncultivated green spaces. On rare occasions one spies a pedestrian here, turning away from the road, seeking a shortcut into the city, or a lost horse meandering slowly, head lowered, nibbling at the grass, peaceful and undisturbed. In the east, one can still make out the ramparts of the citadel where soldiers on watch pace back and forth. Everything is peaceful and still; the noises of the city arrive here as a muted drone, like the babbling of a river.

The world here is free and abandoned: green earth underfoot and a wide open sky overhead, a delight for the eye and a respite for the lungs during the hot, heavy summer days when Nalewki Street boils and heaves, where the only refreshment is a glass of lemonade in a grimy glass, sold by an old Jewish woman in the street.

And here it is that our heroes, Sheker and Shlimazl, have found a place to walk, a place to lie in the grass without being disturbed.

"Who needs the Saxon Garden! With their: *walk here, don't walk there, don't touch that, don't stand there*—Not for us, brother! That's a place for those who like to box everything in, lock everything away, fence it all off. Those people cannot even enjoy a stroll unless

34

it's inside a cage with gates, with guards watching over them. Right here, Shlimazl, is the place for our kind. Lie down, sit and pluck blades of grass, do somersaults if you want, my dear friend, it's a free world! What do you say?"

Sheker held forth in this manner, stretched out on the grass next to his friend, looking toward the west where the fiery sun was setting and small clouds, gilded with purple, drifted past.

Shlimazl frowned. "Say what you like—my blood boils when I think of the Saxon Garden. Not the garden itself, but the shame, the shame of it! Do you know what it means for a person to be thrown out like that?"

As he said this he glanced at his hat on the ground, the same crumpled, worn-out hat the guard had taken such a dislike to.

"A foolish incident, you say? No! It was a lesson for me, an edification. It wasn't the guard who threw me out; it was society itself, sending me a message, reminding me that I'm a poor Jewish man, a waster, good for nothing: *you're not our equal, don't come walking with us!*"

"Come now, Shlimazl, enough talk, to hell with them, to hell with society and all those sad philosophies! Look, over there—the girl is here again today..."

Indeed at that very moment, a female figure turned off the main road and made her way across the meadow toward our two friends—the same person they'd noticed walking here on previous evenings. From afar they could make out the dash of a feather on her hat. She was tall, with a white blouse and a black ribbon around her waist. The figure walked slowly, entirely illuminated by rays of sunlight. From a distance it was a sight to behold. But as she came closer the aura of poverty around her became apparent. Her hat was old; her blouse ill-fitting and not as white as it had seemed; the black ribbon was worn out in places; her young face was dull, tired and sickly, and her gaze was apprehensive. Indeed, she was a beautiful girl of around twenty with a slim figure, a thin waist, fair hair, and large light-colored eyes, but she had also been visibly touched by hardship, hunger and worry . . . In short, for our friends: both an enigma and a fitting companion.

Sheker turned to Shlimazl, "Tell you what, let's make her acquaintance, shall we?"

"Why not?" Shlimazl muttered.

"Well come on then—on your feet!"

But Shlimazl, shy and reserved by nature, did not budge from where he lay on the grass. Sheker sprang up, approached the girl and started up a conversation in the typical Warsaw fashion:

"I beg your pardon, *Fraylin*, do you live around here, if I may be so bold as to ask? It's just that I often see you walking here."

The girl, a little taken aback at first, scrutinized Sheker. Collecting herself, she answered:

"No, I don't live around here. I've come out for a walk to get some fresh air."

"I'm also out for a walk, with my friend over there," said Sheker. "It's a lovely spot; we spend a couple of hours here every day."

"Please, tell me," the girl asked, "would you say the air is fresh here? Do you also come here for the fresh air?"

"No," answered Sheker with a smile, "we're just walking, *Fraylin*; I enjoy a good walk and so does my friend."

"Walking just for the sake of it?" the girl wondered.

It transpired that she was recovering from a recent illness and her doctor had prescribed fresh air.

"So, you've been ill, *Fraylin*?" Sheker asked.

"Yes, I'm almost completely cured."

But her shallow breath and the cough that suddenly interrupted her speech indicated how far that was from the truth.

"I work in a tobacco factory," she said by way of explaining her cough. "The tobacco irritates my lungs. The doctor told me to stop working there, but I think it will pass."

Sheker regarded her with pity. Instead of making the acquaintance of a girl for amusement, he had once again come face to face with misery and poverty. He observed her pale, pretty face, and her thin figure, which poverty had tarnished and sickness had eroded. He thought: "Sister, you're gravely ill and you don't even realize it. That factory will gnaw away at you until you have nothing left to give." He rued the thought that so many of his social interactions were taken up with musings such as these and with that he fell silent.

Meanwhile Shlimazl had come to join them, his hair disheveled (he was ashamed of his hat and so he held it casually in his hand). Sheker introduced him with full honors:

"My friend, Nosn-Note Shlimazl allow me to introduce, *Fraylin* . . . what was your name again?"

"My name is Fayngold, and my Jewish name is Manye."

She was once again a little on edge, put off by the appearance of Shlimazl's hair, gait and figure, but Sheker, who had a good instinct for such things, noticed immediately and said with a laugh:

"Don't be afraid of us, *Fraylin* Manye. We won't do you any harm, God forbid, we're decent people, I assure you."

"Quite decent," Shlimazl agreed, offering his hand to the girl.

And all three of them began to stroll together.

Manye walked in the middle with Sheker on her right side and Shlimazl on her left, holding his hat in his hand, waving it in the air, to give himself an air of roguish confidence.

The sun was setting and in the western sky an image formed of many colors, splattered with red, gilded with pale delicate strands of gold, interwoven with pink and dark blue threads and speckled with dark patches of cloud . . . Sheker trudged gloomily, with a heavy heart. Shlimazl, on the other hand, was in good spirits, amusing himself as best he could with their new acquaintance.

That is how our heros befriended the girl from the tobacco factory, an acquaintanceship that would lead them to new ideas, as we shall see later.

It wasn't until all of Warsaw was twinkling with lights and the field was bathed in complete darkness that they walked the girl home to Bonifraterska Street where she lived in a cellar-apartment, bidding her goodnight like old friends. Afterward, Sheker invited Shlimazl home for tea and they spoke about their new acquaintance. It soon became clear that Shlimazl had been completely charmed by Manye; you could say he'd fallen for her at first sight.

"But what do you think of her?" he asked. "That's what I call a beauty! Did you see her eyes?—She's so sweet and down to earth! I like her a thousand times more than all those bourgeois ladies with their coiffed hair. And she's clever too, I'm telling you, she's really quite clever. I wouldn't expect you to understand . . ."

"Why wouldn't I understand, Shlimazl? Oh I understand all right, brother, I understand all too well!" Sheker joked.

"And I can't stand your jokes," said Shlimazl angrily.

Shlimazl would have abandoned his tea, and stormed out the door then and there if Sheker had not appeased his anger in time with kind words and the prospect of future plans.

"Come winter," he said, "our lives will be quite different. You'll find some new students, and I'll get serious about sitting those exams. We'll make something of ourselves, don't you worry about that, my friend. There's no reason to lose your temper. Why worry when we can be happy? Why get angry, when it can all be good?"

They talked and argued in Sheker's room all night. At dawn, when the light began to flow from the east and pour out over the sky, the two friends shook hands and bid each other good night. Shlimazl went home to sleep in his apartment on Smocza Street, merrily humming a tune to himself, filled with a hope every bit as beautiful as the dawning day.

Sheker on the other hand was left alone in his room, where his mood slumped further into gloominess.

III

Getting to Know a Neighbor

Dark clouds obscured the skies for days on end. When the rain wasn't pouring, accompanied by thunder and lightning, or the city wasn't doused in an endless drizzle, then the clouds simply loured overhead, without budging, seemingly asleep. At the very height of summer the weather had turned cold, wet and dreary. And so our friends stayed at home.

Sheker rose in the morning and did a little work. His job as a property clerk involved recording notes in a ledger with details about new tenants who had moved into the building and those who had moved out. Afterward he read for a while and drank some tea. He then went out into the street but soon came back, and resumed pacing around his room for a while, before returning to his book. In the end he lay on his bed, stretched out to his full length, resting his head on his hands, with the contentment of one who had done a hard day's work, without a worry in the world or a single stain on his conscience.

Time passed. All was quiet and peaceful. Thoughts flowed through Sheker's mind, blood flowed through his veins, and his heart went about its business—but all of this happened of its own accord, and Sheker seemed to have no more control over his own thoughts than he did over the blood flowing in his veins, or the valves beating in his heart. Not his problem.

But then Sheker heard the familiar patter of little mice feet, a sound which had often kept him awake at night. With half-opened eyes he glanced over at his table, which was piled high with books, here and there littered with half-eaten pieces of bread and lumps of sugar. He soon spotted the creature whose noise he knew so well, towards which he harbored strong, not altogether positive feelings, and which he had never laid eyes upon until now. A small, nimble creature with shining eyes and flattened, frightened ears, stood next to a book tinkering with a morsel of bread, timidly at first, its mouth waiting, ears at the ready, its glinting eyes watching Sheker, searching to discern if he was awake or asleep. Its little brain seemed to conclude that the enemy was asleep, and so it set about gnawing the bread with abandon, twisting its long tail in pleasure.

The feast was to its liking.

Sheker lay still, watching intently through half-closed eyes. He was pleased to finally get to know such a close neighbor. There had been no need for such animosity. As if the tiny creature had nothing better to do than to deliberately disturb Sheker's sleep!

"Well, my friend," he said, "you're not at all as ugly as they would have me believe. You just want to live. You eat quietly and want to put one over on me. Well then, let's get to know each other a little better. Even if I'm a human being, and you're just a tiny frightened animal."

41

Thinking this he pulled a detachable cuff—not the cleanest, it must be said—out from inside his shirt-sleeve, then he sat up in bed as quietly as possible and with one quick movement the mouse was captured: surrounded on all sides by a white tower, blocked on top by a human hand, without a single crevice or hole through which to escape.

Bewildered by its unexpected misfortune, the mouse began walking around inside the cuff, before attempting to scale the walls of its new prison. But coming into contact with Sheker's hand, feeling the warmth of human flesh and bones, the mouse was struck with terror, and fell back down, where it resumed turning in circles. Sheker raised his hand a little, to take a peek at his captive neighbor. His gaze only frightened the mouse even more. Seeing the new opening the mouse once again attempted to climb, but Sheker had only to shift his hand again for the mouse to lose all hope of escape.

It was only fortuitous circumstance that allowed the mouse to finally flee its predicament. Shlimazl came to visit his friend, knocked on the door, and as Sheker was distracted, the mouse tipped over the cuff and made good its escape.

"What's the matter?" said Shlimazl, seeing on his friend's face that something had happened.

"I . . . I was studying . . . zoology," Sheker answered hastily, "and you came at just the wrong moment, ruining my experiment!"

Shlimazl glared at him in surprise.

"I don't understand," he said earnestly. "Have you finally gone mad? I've told you it's not good for a person to idle around with nothing to do, with a head full of chaos, with no regard for anything . . ."

"Moralizing again, is it?" said Sheker, waving his hands. "Leave me in peace! I'm not mad; I was studying zoology, there you have it."

And he told him about the mouse.

"Upon my word," Sheker protested good-naturedly, "Upon my word, I don't understand you. How can one be so frivolous, sitting at home catching mice, uninterested in the world?"

Sheker cast his friend a searching glance and asked:

"And what exactly should I be interested in?"

"Why, for example, do you not take the slightest interest in a girl like Manye? She's a poor girl, works all day in the factory, in terrible drudgery, the poor thing, and she is weak, she needs to rest . . ."

"True," Sheker said earnestly, "She is ill."

"Ill," Shimazl muttered and from his tone it was not clear if this was a question or a reproach or if it was a kind of sigh, an expression of his pity.

"But, tell me," Shlimazl continued in a confidential tone, "is she not lovely? A dear, sweet golden heart she has—so sad! Why must a girl like that toil day in day out sacrificing her beauty, her youth . . ."

"You're right about that. But it's not just her beauty and youth that she's frittering away in that factory, but also her health. It has been on my mind."

"Something must be done!" Shlimazl cried out. "Do you know what I'm going to do? I'm going to ask her to stop working."

"But she has to earn a living!"

43

"Don't worry, I'll figure something out. You'll see. And if there's no money, then I'll go and work in the factory myself! You don't think I'm capable of working in a factory? What would be wrong with that?"

"Nothing at all," Sheker answered calmly, "it's no worse than teaching Hebrew lessons or being a property clerk, and it's probably more interesting, you get to work alongside others, get to feel like one of many . . . I've already thought about it."

"Is there anything this fellow hasn't thought about! What comes of all your thinking?"

"Listen, that's what I'm telling you, Shlimazl, I'm a born philosopher, that's what I am! A philosopher, and today I became a biologist too, a zoologist."

"Stop with your jokes, please," Shlimazl said.

"Okay then, what do you intend to do? God damn it, will it ever stop raining?"

And yet, despite the rain, the two friends ventured out into the street.

IV
In the Café

The narrow strip of sky above Franciszkańska Street was filled with gloomy clouds, like a dull mass of thick paint daubed across the sky, expressing nothing and allowing nothing to be heard, save perhaps the old teachings of *Ecclesiastes* that all is vanity: *The sun also ariseth, and the sun goeth down, and hasteth to his place where he arose, The wind goeth toward the south, and turneth about unto the north; it whirleth about continually, and the wind returneth again according to his circuits.* The same thing happens day in day out, year in year out, forever and ever without end. Tedious, senseless raindrops continue to fall and a fog hangs in the air. It seems as though summer has come down with something nasty and is lying unconscious. But down below on Franciszkańska Street, there is bustle and noise; Jews wipe their sweaty brows, perspiring just as much in this rainy weather as they do during a heat wave. The overpowering smell of leather seeps out from every doorway, creeping into one's every sense, like the Plague of Darkness in Egypt, so solid one could reach out and touch it. Here, at the intersection of Wałowa Street, the smell of old clothing adds itself to the mix, and from Bonifraterska Street the wind carries the scent of Tobacco. Heavy trucks packed with leather rattle through the street. Jews in long coats and ritual fringes, with long beards and bulging eyes, run around wheeling and dealing. Two of them collide with each other and glare with the blank eyes of madmen, they gesticulate wildly, each in his own corner, before continuing on their way. And there, a young man with trimmed sidelocks, in a velvet hat, his beard only just beginning to sprout, clearly fresh from living with his in-laws in the provinces and arriving in Warsaw for the first time to find a livelihood. He walks slowly and his dreamy, half-mystical eyes wander, seeking something, while the heaving street thrusts him to the right and to the left and backwards, like a river tossing a twig. The heavens continue to pour down, and it seemed as though hiding in an attic somewhere Ecclesiastes is poking his ancient, wizened face, with cold, ironic eyes out through a hole, gazing down onto Franciszkańska Street and laughing, sticking out his tongue, reciting his old motto: *all is vanity!*

Sheker and Shlimazl ambled together through the street, Sheker leading Shlimazl, talking confidentially, speaking in cryptic shorthand like a pair of lovers. The cacophony of the street was unrelenting, but it did not concern them much: if Sheker missed a word it was enough to look into Shlimazl's face and watch his lips move and all was as good as understood; if Shlimazl did not hear a question, he'd look his friend in the eyes and would understand exactly what he meant. But the frantic passersby jostling them from all sides made Shlimazl lose his patience and scold:

"Wild people, fanatic creatures! How they rush about!"

"Relax, Shlimazl. Those wild creatures are doing something, as you can see; they're supplying the world with leather. You want to wear boots, don't you my friend? Boots without holes even."

Sheker continued: "I have to admit I envy them, those wild creatures. They labor with such enthusiasm, with everything they've got, as if leather were the most important thing in the world. What more does a person need to be happy than to put everything they've got into something? Am I right, Shlimazl?"

"Savages is what they are," said Shlimazl, spitting on the ground. "I can't stand them."

"There's no call for spitting, Shlimazl—I don't approve. These are human beings, and a human being, my good fellow, is the most beautiful and clever animal on this Earth, the most downtrodden and wretched creature of them all. I'm telling you."

So philosophized our pair as they turned into a narrow side street.

"Where are we going anyway?" asked Sheker.

"We're going . . . well, you'll see, there's a café down here we can pay a visit to."

"What for?"

"Well . . . sitting there . . . I don't need to . . . it's just that Manye goes there sometimes."

"Aha, so that's it!" said Sheker. "So that's where you're taking me? In that case there's no need to be bashful. The heart wants what it wants. I'll probably get in your way. You should go ahead without me."

"Don't start with your jokes. You've got the wrong end of the stick. We don't have to go in if you don't want to. It's just that, seeing as we're already here, we might as well stop by."

"After you."

Mounting three steps, our duo pushed open a glass-paneled door, whose panes were no clearer or more transparent than the sky over Franciszkańska Street, then down a step and suddenly the sharp smell of distant leather was replaced by a warm soft cloud of fug and the odor of sweaty walls. The room was divided in two by a Spanish-wall partition. Beyond the partition a large kettle was boiling, filling the entire room with steam. On the near side there were small tables and chairs, and a counter laden with all manner of sweets and cakes, which seemed destined to be devoured, not

only by the customers, but—perhaps more than anything—by the swarm of flies that buzzed around them
with a joyous din. Behind the first room, there was also
a second smaller, darker room where a lamp burned
even during the day. Young people, men and women,
some sitting by the tables and some standing around
them in heated discussion, filled the smaller room. It
was immediately apparent that they were all part of
one group. Sheker and Shlimazl sat down at a table and
ordered tea.

At first the young people did not notice the newcomers. Our friends were also unconcerned with who
they were, or what they were discussing so heatedly.
Shlimazl, impatient for Manye to arrive, sat lost in day-
dreams. Sheker meanwhile took in his new surround-
ings. On the wall he saw a large painting depicting the
span of one sinful human life. On one side, in the lower
corner, was a child; a little higher up was a Jewish boy,
healthy and strong; then a young man in the middle,
taller than the others; beside him a man of around forty, strong and upright. Then, midway through, things
began to degrade: the same figure appeared again, older
this time, increasingly gray and stooped; and finally
at the very bottom, a gray ninety-year old, feeble and
bent, leaning on a walking-stick. Rendered in cheap
materials, and now further obscured by the smudged
black footprints of generations of flies—the painting
had drawn many sighs from Jewish hearts over the
years: A Man, for example, spends a whole summer's
day running around unable to drum up any business; he
can't lay his hands on credit; his feet are aching and he's

on the verge of collapse—he comes into this café, orders a glass of hot tea, washes his hands, and sits down to a couple of warm bread rolls. He glances up at the painting whereupon he suddenly becomes conscious of his graying hair, and the fact that so many years have already passed since his wedding; conscious of how much he has toiled and how many more years of drudgery he has still ahead of him, he lets out a sigh as mournful as the atoning prayers of Yom Kippur. A young man returns after two weeks visiting the Gerer Rebbe, but it is only upon seeing the painting, that he truly feels compelled to go back on the straight and narrow . . . but now, little over a year later, the painting has lost its power. New customers have begun to appear for whom the words of Ecclesiastes and repentant soul searching are alien notions; clients who do not understand the sigh of a broken heart, or the humiliation of a broken spirit. A new generation has been born with a chip on its shoulder and a fire in its eyes . . . The painting still hangs on the wall. Flies have left their stains on it and no one takes any notice. If Sheker had not happened to come in that day no one would have paid it any attention at all.

Afterward Sheker began to observe the other people around him. It was in Sheker's nature that once he had raised his eyes to look at someone he was slow to lower his gaze. He enjoyed looking at a person and observing them at leisure, like one who holds an unusual object in his hands and turns it over to see it from all angles. In this manner he took the measure of everyone there, one after the other until they started to regard him with suspicion, and they began to whisper:

"An informer!"

And then one of the workers, a stocky youth with pockmarks on his face, who was unable to speak quietly, asked in a deep baritone, which Sheker could hear from his table:

"Comrades! Does anyone here have a pistol?"

"Shlimazl, do you know what these workers of yours suspect us of?"

"What do you mean: *of mine*? They're no more mine than they are yours."

"But what do you say to that? They think we're informers! You're the one who brought us here. What are you going to do if you end up getting a bullet in the heart? It might be best, brother, to say your last confession and kiss life goodbye."

As they spoke the whispering at the other table intensified, accompanied by more frequent glances. Shlimazl began to feel genuinely afraid.

"Where is your Manye?" Sheker asked bitterly.

"I fear she won't be coming today. Tell you what, Sheker, let's get out of here."

"No! Not that! Firstly, that would only make things worse, and secondly, let's see what happens. Once you've gotten yourself in a tight spot, brother, the best you can do is stand your ground until the end."

Meanwhile a girl approached them, a beautiful dark-haired creature with intelligent eyes, agile and lively. Someone had whispered a word in her ear and she'd not needed long to appraise the situation before beckoning one of her companions and approaching our heroes' table.

"Let me do the talking, Shlimazl," Sheker said. "I'll show them who they're dealing with."

"You leave me alone!" Shlimazl growled.

"What are you doing here?" the young man asked, turning to Sheker as he reached the table.

Sheker opened his laughing, curious eyes wide and answered:

"I'm drinking tea."

"I can see that. What I want to know is, what is your business? If you catch my meaning: who are you? What are we dealing with here?"

"You're dealing with a person named Sheker, and what manner of person do I have the honor of speaking to?"

Meanwhile the girl began to argue with Shlimazl. She had a sincere voice, steeped in pain, and no matter how harshly she spoke the words always came out gently. She said:

"No more drama! It's a simple matter, and you must excuse us. In short: there are suspicions that you are informers. Tell us who you are and allow yourselves to be searched."

"Searched? With the greatest of pleasures," said Shlimazl. "Whyever not?" Come on then . . ." and he proceeded to unbutton his jacket.

"I won't allow myself to be searched," said Sheker firmly. "I'm no thief, and you're no gendarmes. What gives you the right, I ask you!"

"Allow us, young man." the girl said to him. "It's entirely possible that we are mistaken. But if you're an honest man you'll understand that once suspicion has fallen on you it's up to you to cast it off. No other way. It can happen to anyone these days. Besides, I must say your words do little to convince me of your innocence. On the contrary, they make me suspect you even more."

"Of being an informer?

"I won't say for sure, but at any rate we have reasons to be cautious."

"An informer? Me? Are you not ashamed to treat a person so recklessly? What do you know of the thoughts that pass through my head? What do you know of the feelings in my heart? Me—an informer! Come off it! What an eye you have! You should be ashamed!"

"Perhaps you're right, and perhaps not. You're certainly an intellectual, that much I can hear. Either way, your resistance will do you no good. If you won't allow us to search you, we will do it by force. And I must warn you that you could pay with your life . . ."

As she spoke these words, one of her companions pulled up a trouser leg to reveal a revolver tucked into his boot. There was a moment of silence.

Shlimazl interjected and said:

"Let them search you, you fool . . . what are you doing? You lunatic!"

With that Sheker rose to his feet and bellowed in rage:

"No! In good conscience I cannot submit myself to such humiliation! They want to threaten me with death? If you don't mind me asking, *Fraylin*, what makes you think my life has any value to me? Perhaps I have spit on life a thousand times? . . ."

"Tell you what," said Shlimazl, falling on a plan, "if you don't want them to search you, fine. I'll search you while they watch, and that'll be an end to it. They'll trust me and there'll be no shame in it for you."

"Listen, my dear friend," Sheker answered with mocking anger, "I may be fond of you, and yet I say—back down!"

At this the worker with the deep voice stood up and said:

"Look at this fool! Let me at him!"

A pair of strong hands grabbed Sheker by the collar and he fell silent. Other hands began patting down his pockets.

In the middle of this scene the door opened and in came a fair haired woman with large, light-colored eyes—it was Manye. In surprise, her great big eyes grew even larger. Shlimazl cried out like someone being rescued:

"Manye!"

She gave him her hand and remained standing in bewilderment.

"Manye, these are your acquaintances, they suspected us of . . . tell them . . ." and his eyes were filled with tears.

The misunderstanding was soon put straight, and in a few short minutes everyone had become good friends. The girl asked for Sheker's forgiveness and smiled at him knowingly. Shlimazl and Manye sat together at a table, his face glowing with pleasure. With smitten eyes he gazed at the simple beauty of that sickly creature in front of him, tentatively touching her hands now and then.

"What a shame," Sheker said calmly, "after all that my tea's gone cold. Landlord, a hot glass of tea if you would!" He was silent for a moment before continuing: "What do you say, Shlimazl? You've decided to live after all? Probably for the best, I won't eat my heart out—life is life. You know what, Shlimazl? Whatever the philosophers decide about which is better, life or death, one thing is clear: no one should be scared of either one, not of life and not of death . . ."

Sheker fell silent and looked at the painting hanging on the wall.

This is what he thought:

The artist should have painted a dead man in the grave beside the ninety-year old. A second-rate artist! Approaching the end he lost his nerve and was frightened by his own idea, he stopped short before seeing it through . . . how frail is the human race! . . .

V
Sheker Alone

Sheker was left all alone in the world. With each passing day his only close friend, Shlimazl, was growing more distant. One day he stopped him on the street, intending to spend time with him as they usually did, but Shlimazl twisted out of his grip and announced with a grave face that he had no time.

"Why so busy? What new business do you have?" Sheker asked.

But Shlimazl ignored the question with an expression of one who has an important secret to hide.

"Why don't you answer?" Sheker continued. "A conspiracy? Politics? Spill the beans, maybe I'll be . . ."

Hearing these words a faint, stifled smile appeared on Shlimazl's lips. He looked down on his friend with a contemptuous gaze, and said politely:

"We'll manage without you. We're not looking for any help."

"Who's this *we*? What group do you belong to? Tell me, Shlimazl . . ."

"Well, I'd better be off. I have no time to chat to you."

And with that he left his friend standing in the street, and strode off with long steps.

Another time—this was in the evening—Sheker was trudging along Franciszkańska Street, feeling so melancholy he wanted nothing more than to close his eyes and drift off to sleep forever. As he was walking like this who should he spot in the distance, coming toward him, but Shlimazl and Manye. Shlimazl held Manye by the arm like a good cavalier, speaking into her ear. He was animated, speaking with ardor, his face all but bathed in pleasure. His frail, feminine companion, however, seemed uninterested in the conversation, and from afar she smiled to Sheker with her eyes. Naturally, seeing two acquaintances like this lifted Sheker's spirits. He sighed as though setting down a heavy burden, and approached them with a smile, ready to embrace them joyfully, but then—woe! He was visited by bitter disappointment—a frequent guest in such a volatile heart as Sheker's. Shlimazl greeted him with a sour frown, and offered his hand with such estranged coldness, that Manye, noticing her cavalier's reaction, felt unsure what to do, or how to behave. Her clear eyes took on a gloomy air. The joy in Sheker's eyes gave way to a flame of anger.

"So you don't recognize me anymore, old boy! Is that it? Oh how I'd love to box the tip of your red little nose! If it wasn't for your lady friend, believe me, I'd do it, Shlimazl. Fare well, then, I don't want to know you anymore..."

Thus he poured out his bitterness and wrath, ending once and for all a friendship of many years.

It was late at night when Sheker arrived home; his eyes were coated in a layer of tears that seemed to lack the courage to flow; and his heart was filled with such a mass of desolation that one could ration it to darken years of life and happiness. He approached the mirror and looked into the face of this new Sheker: alone in the world, whom no living soul wanted to know, surprised by the rosy-faced figure in the mirror, seeking the mystery behind his loneliness. In the end he stuck his tongue out at himself—a gesture intended to include the whole world and all the people in it, Manye and Shlimazl included—he undressed and prepared for a long, sleepless night...

"What have I accomplished?" he thought, biting his lip, tossing and turning in bed. "I have killed every feeling in my heart. For years I have studied the art of apathy, the art of not wanting, and I believed myself to be invulnerable, because I had nothing left to lose—what have I accomplished if such a wretched nobody with such a small head, can, with nothing more than a sour expression, destroy me, causing every part of me to rise up against myself? It would seem I have not yet tried everything. There is more to come. . . The devil take him! Let them come, those new torments . . . Am I incapable of suffering?—Onwards! I'll close my eyes and keep going, wherever the current takes me! . . ."

Meanwhile, during the same period as our Sheker was shutting himself away from the world, a revolution was awakening in the attics and cellar-rooms, home to the clients of drudgery and adversity. Throngs of young people, men and women, pale and nervous, filled the evening streets of the Jewish quarter. Scores and scores of them were snatched up and led to the police stations and prisons, but, like the sea, the crowd did not exhaust itself; its agitation did not let up, but intensified with each passing day, building to a storm. The people looked different, they had a different soul, and like a shadow Sheker wandered among them, isolated and alienated from everyone and everything, not understanding what was in the air, or what would come of it all.

"The thread of my life has snapped," he thought during those days. "What will happen, what will happen?" . . .

And most terrible of all was the thought that his great loneliness all stemmed from such a miserable pin-headed wretch as Shlimazl.

One evening as he wandered the streets, the fiery circle of the setting-sun shone from a westward side-street.

It hovered there silently, like the lucid, knowing, celestial eye at the furthest edge of the heavens; flaming rods spread over the hats of the youths, and glinted in the hair of the girls who were strolling as usual, whispering important, earnest, exciting things to one another. And it seemed to Sheker as though the whole crowd stared at him with suspicion. The looks he received seemed to say: "Watch out, watch out, there goes an informer!" He was sure that they fell silent just as he was passing. He ran home, to his cramped room where a desolate melancholy began to prowl amid the evening shadows.

For several days he could not stop fixating on the mental image of a hook upon the wall, and a length of rope.

He sat like that in the dark, both hands on his knees, his head slumped forwards, his hair disheveled, with one earnest thought in his mind. A bright star shone in through his window, winking down from the wide world . . . so silent and lovely was the thin beam, a shame one cannot take it inside where the darkness is so unending! . . .

He sat in this position for a long time until finally a creak from the door snapped him out of his reverie.

It was Shlimazl and Manye. They entered, out of breath. They were terrified and had clearly been running.

Shlimazl, attempting to make light of the situation, struck a pose and declared in a formal tone:

"It appears I need to exploit the memory of our old friendship in order to save myself and Manye from danger." He gestured toward Manye who lay a packet of forbidden literature down on the table. "The police got wind of us and are on our tail. I hope you have courage enough to let us wait here until the coast is clear."

"This is unexpected," Sheker said, as though to himself. "Fine then, fine, we'll be friends again. What is it *Fraylin* Manye? Why have you turned so pale? . . ."

1905

A NIGHT IN THE FIELD
From the writings of a madman

I

... I stand in the middle of a field, looking at the sun ...

And the sun grows ever larger and redder, moving across the rolling sky to set in the west. Its final rays burn my eyes like a fire. But I cannot, do not wish to avert my eyes—from that beautiful, red sun.

A fierce desire compelled me to leave the city and come here. "Come, let us go out to the fields," my heart whispered to me. "There you will see the sun go down, and you will recognize the true border between day and night."

In the city everything is jumbled. Towering walls obscure the sky at dawn and at dusk. If a person were to approach me at sundown, grab me by the shoulders and demand: "Tell me, you little fool, which is it: night or day?" I would not know the answer and would be forced to hold my tongue in shame.

I have brought a bell with me, and when I can no longer see the sun I shall ring the bell: It is night!

Should I fear the dark clouds? Lest they swallow up the sun, preventing me from seeing, from knowing?

No! These dogged clouds are also sorrowful. For I have spoken to them, passing many pleasant hours; they understand me, and know my thoughts.

Understanding me, knowing me as they do, they must surely love me.

Why would those good clouds wish to cause me anguish?

We stare directly at one another: I into the sun's crimson face, and the sun into my wan face. The lower the sun plunges, the narrower grows that thin band of sky between sun and earth.

They embrace: the orb of the sun kisses the unhappy earth.

And my heart calls out: Flee from here, sun. Tomorrow, before dawn I shall be standing by the east, waiting for you to rise.

The instant the sun appears I shall ring the bell: It is day!

I hold the bell ready in my hand. But at that very same moment a nimble little black cloud approaches . . . there it is—it covers up my sun.

I fall to the ground, and my heart asks: "Oh, my good sun, what am I doing here on this wide earth?"

But my sun has been devoured by a miniature devil riding on a swift cloud, and I am left all alone by myself in the field with a bell in my hand.

II

I lie prostrate on the ground, my face buried in the soil, and I weep.

It's not my eyes that weep, but my heart.

My limbs feel weakened and unhitched, but there is life in them yet.

They wish to live, but live by their own reckoning, not under the yoke of my frail, diseased mind.

Only my heart is alive! It hears and feels and thinks. My heart controls everything inside me.

My brain is empty of every thought. Now and then a stray idea flashes through, but it invariably disappears a moment later.

Disparate images are hounded by queer thoughts through my mind.

In the prayer house behind a bench—*omar Abaye*... a bird is burned by the breath from my mouth, falling from the sky to the earth. Its soul thanks me that I have freed it from purgatory.

In the garden, cherry lips on pale cheeks. My lean fingers cradle a tangle of raven hair which tumbles over her shoulders.

And a fire rages within my every limb.

The girl lies in the cemetery, on a grave. I lift a corner of her white shroud and place the clay shards onto her eyes, her dull eyes without a vestige of luster.

In the big city I pass through the gate and stop for a moment. The street is teeming: unhappy wretches!

They do not know their own lives. Surging, they appear to chase each other . . . but whither? To what end? Where is the great precipice to which all the currents are drawn? . . .

Where is the truth? . . .

"Curse God and man, curse the world and all that's in it!" I hear a voice beside me.

Two sable wings unfurl above me: it is Satan with a black, fiery crown upon his head, standing by my side.

"Curse them?" I scream with all my strength. ". . . I may not!"

And with that, he is gone.

III

With a thousand shining eyes the heavens behold the earth. Proudly they hold up the Moon and, pointing towards the earth, they say to it: "Just gaze upon my riches, my beautiful crown!"

Woe to you, foolish sky! You have worn the sun upon your head, the great beautiful sun. And now it is lost to you; just wait till it rises for you again!

Am I not, then, cleverer than you, inscrutable sky? When I lost the girl, my angel, my crown—did I seek out dolls in human form to play with in her staid?

From that time on I have walked in shadow, waiting for my sunrise—when I will find the truth.

I must find it, whatever it may be!

"Weak boy," my heart hears a voice cry out. Where the heavens and the earth come together, there you will find your truth. Stand up and see:

To the west, where the sky embraces the earth, a large hand appears; it beckons to me and I hear:

"Approach, small child, here is the truth—when God created the world the heavens and earth fought one another; each wanted the truth for itself. And so God hid the truth in the middle, between earth and sky. Come here and you will see for yourself!"

And I walk.

But the spot where the heaven embraces the earth remains ever out of reach; the hand beckons and beckons, pulling me as though with enchanted ropes.

My head protests, crying angrily: "Why are you walking? Do you think you can ever arrive at your destination?"

But my heart drives me onward to where heaven and earth come together, to where the truth lies.

And I walk.

IV

I am weary from my long journey, yet the hand continues to beckon and call.

O God! He wants to oppress me. The great God toys with me thus and revels in oppressing me, weak, sick child that I am, who will one day cease to be.

"Sick child," I hear a voice say from behind me.

It is an old man with white hair who has called my name.

White as snow are his locks, his frame is imposing and as straight as a palm; he approaches me with measured steps and lays his hand upon my shoulder.

"You seek the truth, child?"

"Old man! You know it, do you not?" I kiss his feet.

"You are tired, child. Sit with me for a moment and listen to my tale. I have a fine tale to tell."

"Tell me the truth!" I cry out loud in annoyance. "I shall pluck the hairs from your beard . . ."

"Child," he says calmly, "the truth can wait, this is eternity. And your time is come to an end."

And he recounts:

"There was once a head of cabbage, and when it was still fresh and whole, a family of worms came to colonize it. Where the worms came from, I do not know."

"O, wretched old man!" I cry. A hundred years you've lived and you still don't know?"

He appeases me and continues:

"The worms in the cabbage lived, were fruitful and perished. Much time passed and from that one family grew many families, but they did not live in harmony. I do not know why. A thousand days passed and much time sank into the black abyss.

"Upon that green cabbage, melancholy worms were born and those worms had long sharp horns. And with those horns they dug holes into the cabbage: they wished to know what lay underneath.

Suddenly there was turmoil on the cabbage head. One of the melancholy worms held a speech:

"'Brothers, o brothers, what are we doing? We sit on the outer skin of the cabbage, but not on the cabbage itself. That is why we are so cramped, which is why we fight one another. Come brothers, let us tear the skin asunder. Let us sit on the cabbage itself. Brother, o my brothers! . . .'

"The speaker was pelted with stones. 'He aims to destroy the world,' they cried.

"But two more worms arrived to take the place of the dead one. And those, too, were killed, and again more came to take their place. And so it went. No doubt you can count, boy.

"And they tore up the cabbage skin, and sang songs of liberation.

"Much time passed, and again there was a tumult on the cabbage skin.

"Another long-horned worm spoke and it too was stoned to death.

"More followed and layer after layer of skin was exposed. The speakers wished to get to the very core, the truth of the cabbage head."

"Oh, you vile old fool," I cry aloud. "It was Satan who sent you to me."

"I am a man."

"And what do you want here? Here where I seek the truth?"

"Look, child, and see," he says. "It is a clear summer's night and I love to walk. It is what I am accustomed to."

"Villainous old man!" I bellow. "In the woods beyond, Death is waiting. He's coming for you."

Hearing these words the old man's face turned ashen, and he fell dead to the ground.

V

How long the night drags on!

An easy, clear breeze blows and whispers in my ear:

"The sun will soon be here..."

Will I live to see the dawn? And if I die, will I fall with my face pointed toward the sky so that the rising sun may at least look down upon my pallid countenance?

My heart says to me:

"You will die, and fall face down onto the earth; and the sun will never know who, or what, lies on the ground!"

And yet, how I do love the sun!

No! I shall not die, I shall not die until I can sing my song for the great beautiful sun!

My song will be carried aloft: the song of a dying man for the sun!

1910

IN A JEWISH SHOP

There is a burning frost and a strong wind. The flames in the street-lanterns flicker and with each gust of wind we feel—my companion and I—as though the skin on our faces has been stung by a potent venom. We are hastening homeward, to our warm room. But I remember that I've run out of cigarettes and so I am keeping an eye out for an open shop.

"There's a shop," I say, addressing my companion. "I'm just going to go in and pick up some cigarettes."

"Hurry, though!" My friend is not happy.

"Come in with me," I invite him, "why should you freeze out here?" I say, knowing full well that the frost is not bringing him any joy.

"Go and come back quickly!" He says in an authoritative tone, stammering from the cold, "hu—rr—ry!"

I know my friend and am familiar with his aversion to going into a house or a shop with someone when he himself has no business there. To submit to being dragged along by a friend is not in his nature.

I go inside. And as I close the door behind me, I observe my friend hopping on his feet which are already cold from the frozen pavement.

A good-hearted lad, I think to myself, no fool, lively and joyous . . . but pale and weak, skinny, without a drop of blood, like most of us youngsters, he shivers violently in the cold—the true sign of weak blood. When I come out I'll advise him to take some fish oil . . .

I glance at the crate of cigarettes: an unholy mess! Red, white, green, and blue packets lying all over the place, as if a battalion of mice had been fighting a war there, leaving behind disruption and disorder . . .

Behind the counter stands the shopkeeper: a short, gray-haired Jew wearing a crumpled velvet hat, and a thick, half-silk belt around a long black gaberdine. In the other corner, next to the cigarettes, stands his wife, a woman aged before her time, knitting a sock. By the counter, shivering with cold, stands a ten-year-old girl, rubbing her half-frozen hands together.

"A ten-pack of Kabinets," I say.

The shopkeeper straightens himself up, takes his hands out of his pockets, and with that drawn-out Varsovian intonation, asks:

"Whha'?"

I repeat my request.

"Cigarettes?" he asks, a tinge of astonishment in his voice, "what kind?"

I repeat once again the name of the brand, endeavoring to raise my voice; I have not forgotten about my friend outside, shivering in the cold.

"Kabinets?" he asks me again with growing astonishment, as if I had told him that the Behemoth itself was outside, stalking the streets. "Sureh!" He calls out to his wife, "hurry up and give this gentleman a packet of cigarettes!"

I approach the shopkeeper's wife, and wait with baited breath. Through the ice-encrusted window I spy a figure striding impatiently up and down and I surmise that by now my friend is well and truly angry with me.

I want to rush to the door to beckon him inside, but at that moment the woman puts down her knitting and raises her eyes to make contact with mine—progress!

The exchange begins again from the beginning:

"What can I get for you?"

"Ten Kabinets . . ."

"Kabinets?" she repeats, in a quieter voice, as though speaking in her sleep.

"Kabinets, Kabinets, I don't have all day!" I say, beginning to lose my temper.

I look the woman in the eyes: God how much stupidity and how much pain!

"Have mercy," I beg her, "just give me the cigarettes! Someone's waiting for me, there's such a bitter frost outside . . ."

"A bitter frost," she interrupts me, "this time last year, it was still warm, a hard winter . . ."

I fear her monologue may be a long one. Any minute now she's going to start talking about the terrible frost in Siberia, and about the war that's threatening to break out . . . and I implore her:

"For pity's sake, give me the cigarettes. I don't have time . . ."

"Kabinets," she says again, with the intonation of a question and answer in one, approaching—or so I hope—the place where the cigarettes are kept.

I can't make out what was going on back there, but I hear the cigarette packets fall and a voice calling out to the half-frozen girl.

"Khanele! Come over here and pick up these cigarettes . . ."

And to her husband she says, a little scornfully: "Where did you put the Kabinets? You can never find anything here . . ."

"Leave it out!" cries the shopkeeper, "I would have found them by now if you'd get out of my way."

I have half a mind to just leave then and there, but the following scene stops me in my tracks:

The shopkeeper and his wife come together—miraculously managing to find a space to convene in a narrow corner between the counter and the wall—clearly intent on discussing some private matter. Then, just as miraculously, the girl succeeds in squeezing past them. She looks at me for a moment with palpable sympathy, clearly she understands my anger more than her parents do. Speedily she pushes them both aside, and reaches out to hand me the cigarettes. The father holds her back and, standing aside, begins to reprimand his impetuous daughter:

"I don't know what's gotten into this one, the little imp!"

"Am I going to get my cigarettes, or not?" I ask with feigned anger, in order to bring the uncomfortable scene to an end.

"What kind?" The shopkeeper asks again.

"Kabinets."

"Kabinets?"

"Kabinets."

"Five?"

"Ten, I want ten."

"Ten?"

"Ten. And let that be the end of it."

Husband and wife begin searching for the cigarettes, and if it wasn't for the skill of the girl they would probably still be looking for them.

She will grow up and become a good shopkeeper, I think.

You can imagine for yourself the condition I find my friend in; he has been struck dumb with the cold and just about manages to contain his rage. It is only as we arrive home that he begins to complain:

"You'd have to be without a shred of compassion or reason to leave someone waiting so long in the cold!" He has no desire to hear my defence and stands by his words: "Someone with compassion and reason wouldn't have done such a thing."

I think to myself: It appears the frost wasn't messing around with you, my dear friend! But if, like me, you'd seen the shopkeeper and his wife, if you'd seen what was going on behind that counter, you wouldn't be angry. I'm telling you, it's worth freezing in worse frosts than this to witness such a scene!

1912

ALONE

A weak light flickers in the cramped basement room, crawling, as though dispirited and ashamed, from the ramshackle table. Smoke rises from the little lamp. The cracked glass is held together by a sheet of paper, which casts a black shadow over the room, covering part of the floor and reaching halfway up the wall.

An old, worn-out Jew stands by the table mending a nightshirt. He turns it over, pushing it back and forth across the table, his old rheumy eyes following the movements of his own hands. Sometimes he pauses, holding the nightshirt with both hands to prevent it from slipping down onto the floor. He presses it firmly to the table and pauses for a moment.

Is he daydreaming?

His gaze wanders a while over the bare walls of the room, lingering momentarily on his yellowing bedsheets. He turns to the other bed and there his wandering gaze stops, as if drawn by a magnet. His eyes grow wider, and it seems some powerful hidden feeling has flared up inside them: a flash of anger sparks under his brows.

It's as though the old man is attempting to sigh, but even such a simple act is beyond his powers.

He walks a few paces from the table, shuffling his feet, his dirty boots plodding on the floor. He stops suddenly in the middle of the room, as though straining to remember what he is looking for, why he stood up from the table. He returns to his workbench, and to his nightshirt, as if it were capable of distracting him from his loneliness.

He pulls open a drawer, removes a needle, and prepares a black thread. He tries to thread the eye of the needle, but his hands shake and the thread stubbornly resists: it simply refuses to go through.

He then attempts to tease a little more light out of the lamp; the flame begins to leap up and down transferring its movements to the shadows, which dance wildly around the room, here climbing as far as the rafters, there coming down as far as the floor.

The old man picks up the lamp with trembling hands, inspecting it for a moment. The lamp is empty; the flame is going out.

"Hmm," he mumbles an indistinct question between his blue lips and places the lamp back down on the table.

What to do? The question suddenly forms in his mind. "What to do?" he asks himself, aloud this time, observinging the floundering light; the glare has blinded his eyes, and his brow twitches with each bound of the flame.

His wandering eyes once more glance at his bed.

Should he sleep? It's long overdue, it seems, well past midnight. But a shudder passes through his old limbs at the thought of going to bed.

For three nights he has tossed and turned, unable to get any rest. How terrible are the long nights for the lonely old man in his bed! They stretch on and on without end; he turns over in vain, in vain he squeezes his eyes shut—he cannot sleep, though his eyes sting with fatigue.

Three nights, three endless, dark nights have passed since tragedy struck, since his only daughter disappeared. Gone God knows where, to some far off land. And with whom? To what end? No. His old brain is unable to contemplate it. All he knows is that he is alone, all alone in the world. He feels a heavy weight dragging his face and his eyes down toward the floor . . .

Dull but terrible is the pain that has wrenched his heart these past three days.

But last night was the most terrible, dark and interminable of all. He got up several times, shuffling around the room before he wearied and returned to bed until . . . until God had mercy on him and the dull light of morning began to creep in through the dirty windowpanes and he could finally get dressed and go out into the streets . . .

Terrible is the thought of going to bed. And so he has, to keep himself occupied, found some task to do that he would otherwise not have bothered with. The nightshirt is an ancient garment of his, which wouldn't fetch a single groschen at the Wałowa flea market.

But the kerosene is running out and he . . . Oh what to do? What to do? He grumbles manically to himself, clutching the nightshirt in his hands.

Fifteen years previously, another misfortune had visited him: his wife had died after a long illness. They'd had to sell the sewing machine to pay for the doctors and so he went from being a proper tailor to being a mere patcher of old clothing. But at least he hadn't been alone: his wife had left behind a child, the apple of his eye, his daughter Sorele. She was a respectable girl who was training at the workshop on Wałowa Street to learn the ready-to-wear clothing business. A few years after her mother's death she was earning two, later three, four rubles a week. True, the work wasn't easy; she was paid by the piece—three kopecks for a pair of trousers, twenty pairs a day! The little family was poor but happy ... Sorele was a lively and carefree girl, and the old man enjoyed listening to her singing cheerful little songs in the evenings while she cooked dinner, or after the Shabbes meal when Sorele's friends would come to visit, and she would dance with them. The old man could watch for hours from his bed as Sorele danced; she was in command. He smiled and often thought to himself that he was contented ... true, he reproached himself that he was living off his daughter's dowry ... but no one can be completely happy ... and then suddenly an unexpected misfortune befell him.

Sorele and two other girls from the workshop on Wałowa Street had vanished ... There were rumors they had been taken ... one of the girls had been found; her father—a wealthy man—had succeeded in tracking her down, intercepting her at the border just in time. The girl had managed to pass on a message from Sorele for her father telling him not to worry; telling him that everything would be okay ...

Three days and three nights he paced around the room, devastated, mumbling to himself, "Don't worry, don't worry!" The word seemed to have lost all meaning to him:

"*Worry*?... I shouldn't *worry*?"

He repeated this a hundred times, rubbing his brow, unable to understand.

Weak and dulled, his old head tried to imagine life without his daughter: a dark abyss lay before him, and he was staggering toward it on weary feet. He felt that, by leaving, she had also taken half of his soul away, that he had been left half dead.

The light bounces ever higher, assaulting his old, sleep-deprived eyes. He turns around and is paralysed with fright: the dancing shadows confuse him and he struggles to understand what is happening. He cannot remember . . . Suddenly he makes for the door; he has to escape, but then he remembers the paper attached to the broken glass of the lamp, and he lets go of the door handle.

He sits down by the table, leaning his head in his hands, deep in thought, staring at the flickering light. It is shrinking, yet it seems to be bounding with more energy and haste than before. He sees how the flame wrestles, struggles. It wants to keep shining—"Hmm," he mumbles, there isn't enough kerosene. Half formed questions hover in his mind:

What does the flame want? Why is it struggling?...

He closes his eyes and listens to the spluttering lamp; he has a strange feeling that perhaps the flame derives some satisfaction from its struggle . . . Finally the noise stops and he opens his eyes: Everything has gone pitch black, except for a red dot on the wick, and a straight column of smoke pouring out of the glass . . .

"Extinguished,"—he mumbles, as if in a dream, and he imagines he can hear a voice whisper in his ear: *floundered in vain, struggled for nothing! . . .*

1900

SUDDEN OLD AGE

The previous winter had cast a cloud of melancholy over the inhabitants of Toshlin. All roads leading to the small town were hidden in the snow, and many coachmen had strayed from those roads and were lost. In the surrounding hamlets, it was said, hungry wolves came out at night, assailing anyone they encountered. Somewhere in the forest the municipal clerk and his whole family had been murdered by bandits. Farmers were reluctant to venture into town, and so the shops stood empty; the town was dismal and lifeless.

That winter hit Shmuel Kotsker hardest of all, though he was no stranger to hunger and cold. In all his years barely a day went by where he hadn't been in desperate need of a guilder or two. He was a *Shadkhn*, a matchmaker, but—if the local prayer house gossip was to be believed—he had never successfully arranged a marriage in his entire career. Nevertheless, he earned a little something from every betrothal. Whenever a match was being arranged in the town, and the process was sufficiently advanced for it to be a matter of common knowledge, then Shmuel Kotsker would approach the father of the prospective bride or groom, lead him aside and whisper in his ear—suggesting the very same match that had already been arranged. The father-in-law to be, if he wasn't a complete fool, understood that it was best to hold his tongue. The standard procedure, as everyone knew, was to slip a coin or two into Shmuel Kotsker's hand, whereupon he would grumble and curse about the paltriness of his commision. The townsfolk had long grown used to Shmuel's oaths and protestations. The gabbay who ran the prayer house, from whom Shmuel regularly accepted alms, was already so accustomed to hearing Shmuel's volley of epithets that he barely noticed it anymore, he would stand there discussing business with his wife, while Shmuel swore, stamped around, pounded his fists on the table, and generally made a great commotion: "I'm a Hasid, don't forget, a follower of the Kotzker Rebbe, I deserve some respect!". . . But there was nothing to be done. In the end he would pocket the two guilders and take his leave. But for Shmuel Kotsker there was nothing trivial about these outbursts; on each occasion he felt offended anew, growing agitated, waging an endless war against everyone and everything. So he lived for many years, unaware that he was growing old, or that he was living at all . . . It all felt to him like a preparation, an inconvenience to be endured before he could begin his life in earnest. Then, last winter, he grew increasingly feeble and the cold crept deeper into his bones. The final straw came when the townsfolk discovered his true age—Shmuel Kotsker was seventy years old.

The truth came to light when his son was brought before the Tsarist military draft board and the conscription officers read out the family details from the ledger in a clear voice: "*Shmuel Yankelyevitch—syemdyesat lyet.*" The whole town learned the secret that Shmuel had been hiding even from himself, and the revelation was so unexpected that the townsfolk could talk of nothing else. No one could have imagined that the nimble, spirited man—with a beard of indeterminate hue, neither obviously gray, nor stained—Shmuel who was always rushing about, starting arguments, who never ceased agitating for even a moment, was already a septuagenarian, an old man who should by rights command a little respect.

"Well, Shmuel, I hear you're already an old man? Well I'll be!" they greeted him at the prayer house.

"What a story!" another said in amazement. "We should stand up for you when you enter the room!"

Wherever he went he was met with such remarks. He tried to laugh it off and change the subject, figuring they would forget about it soon enough and everything would go back to normal.

He was mistaken.

When they saw him running across the street they were impressed and called out:

"Just look at the old fellow go!"

When he cursed and bellowed at everyone they reminded him of his age. And when they noticed that he did not like to talk about it, they make jokes at his expense: "What's there to be ashamed of?" a young man at the prayer house said one time. "There's nothing wrong with being old, is there Shmuel? Though why that beard of yours isn't gray is a question!" As he said this he grabbed Shmuel's beard in an overly familiar manner. At a different time or in a different context it would not have occured to Shmuel to be offended; this time however he fell into a terrible rage and screamed: "You insolent brat! Delinquent! Where does a child like you get the nerve to grab an old Hasid like me by the beard? A beating is what you'll get! Out of this prayer house right now, you swine!"

Naturally, the affair would have ended in a beating if the others had not held Shmuel back by force. In the end it was agreed the young man should make amends with a bottle of brandy, and so they raised their glasses, drank to Shmuel's health, and wished him a long life.

That winter Shmuel's disposition soured and he could no longer find his place in the world. Everything had changed; people spoke to him differently, he answered differently.

Young people began to address him with a level of formality he was unaccustomed to. The gabbay no longer remained silent when Shmuel cursed and shouted, but instead tried to humor him with kind words.

"What can one do, Reb Shmuel? There's nothing to be done, you understand well enough yourself."

But this new tone did not sit well with Shmuel. He did not know how to respond to it, and he was by no means prepared to play the role of an old man. With each passing day he felt increasingly despondent. His legs still bore him swiftly; he wanted to rush, run, and shout as usual, but suddenly he remembered that he was an old man in his seventies and his forces simply abandoned him in an instant. The realization made his arms and legs feel heavy and lazy, his voice weak, and so he would sigh deeply.

Where and how had he spent all those seventy years? The question nagged him without let up: "If only I could remember?"

But dredging his memories only brought to the surface images of destitution, cold, screaming children, aggravation, bellowing, curses from his two dead wives, and ceaseless scrambling to find a guilder with no time to stop and worry about the World to Come.

During those long winter nights he attempted to read a page of the Gemara and discovered a terrible secret: he had forgotten, or perhaps never even knew, how to study the holy books.

Winter weighed down on the village like a heavy burden. No one took an interest in Shmuel; no one noticed that his face was growing yellower from day to day, and his body more bent. He took to begging for coins for his dinner. Quietly and calmly, he would ask, and often people would quickly and calmly tell him "no." He attempted to get angry like in the old days, but the words came out in the wrong tone, eliciting only strange looks. On many nights he went home to his terribly cold house without a bite to eat; the sword of the Angel of Death was hanging in the air.

And then one morning Shmuel was nowhere to be found. He had left town in his old age to live out his final years in wandering and deprivation.

1905

PUNISHMENT
(A Fairy Tale)

For years on end the surrounding lands had been dev-astated by war. In the city many had fallen to hunger and pestilence. The rich had buried their possessions and gone into hiding in their cellars, eating dried bread that was sold by weight at the price of gold. The masses screamed, rising up and perishing in their thousands and no one bothered to bury the dead. A poisoned wind blew over the city.

Death stared each person in the eye.

Shmaye the Wise encountered Brakhye the Wise on the street and asked him where he was going.

"I'm going out to the fields. The air is cleaner out there, the sun warmer, and if you die there the soft grass will be your resting place."

Shmaye furrowed his brow, and, after a moment of contemplation, replied:

"Come, let us go together. If one is to die of hunger, it makes no difference if it is in the city or in a field."

With weary footsteps they arrived at distant mead-ows and desolate fields, abandoned and overgrown.

The sun set in the west, plunging the world into darkness.

The two wise men lay down on the grass, their faces glowing in the last flickers of fiery sunlight.

Bit by bit their strength faded, and one spoke to the other in a distant voice, as though from sleep:

"Brakhye, are you asleep, and do your ears hear?"

"I am alive, Shmaye, and I am listening. I drifted into slumber. My ear was pressed against the ground and I heard a tremulous-sweet song coming from the bowels of the earth. All the generations resting in the depths, all the potential lives, which lie hidden, waiting to be born, sang a song while the sun was setting."

"What you say is wonderous, Brakhye, for I too slumbered, my ear pressed against the earth, but heart-rending sobs where what I heard coming out of the depths; all the dead, fading generations resting in the bowels of the earth, crying bitterly in their desolation, while the sun went down. I thought the darkness had settled forever over my eyes until I began to call out your name and I perceived that I was still alive."

Meanwhile, the blackness of night had crept in. There were no stars in the sky. The world held its breath. Only distant flashes, unnatural noises, and the call of trumpets indicated that a war was raging not far away.

The two wise men sensed the proximity of death; an icy chill spread through their limbs.

Brakhye said to Shmaye:

"Can you move your body? Let us try to move so that our bodies face eastward, for that is where the sun will rise again and the golden light of dawn will enliven our skin, which is as yellow and dry as parchment, with bright colors."

Shmaye responded:

"By the time the sun comes up we will be long dead, Brakhye. What do we care about the sun, what do we care of the play of bright colors? Death brings everything to an end."

Brakhye did not answer; he only thought:

Dawn will return the treasures of light and life to the earth; I will turn my body towards it.

With the last of his energy, yearning for light and life, he slowly shifted his dying body until his face was pointed toward the east.

His heart gave one final twitch, and beat its last.

Brakhye lay dead, waiting for the sun, but Shmaye remained, and the icy cold spread through his limbs. Suddenly a regiment of troops on horseback arrived. They lit torches. One of them gave Shmaye's body a kick.

"Stand up, you wastrel, you civilian flea, help us to bury the dead."

"I am the wise man Shmaye. I am dying on the field together with my friend Brakhye the Wise. Leave me alone."

In place of an answer he received another blow. A shovel was placed in his hand. The hot breath of war brought him to his feet, and he buried bodies until dawn.

Then he watched from afar as bright colors traced the peaceful face of his dead friend—and he burst into tears like an infant.

1919

86

HAPPINESS
(A Fairy Tale)

Through infinite space, through the immensity of the cosmos, there flew an angel.

For many long years he had not rested his wings; for many long years he had flown and flown without pause. Whenever he encountered a sun or a star or a lost comet, he would stop and ask: "Excuse me, please. Do you perhaps know where I can find the Earth?"

And on hearing the answer, "no," he would fly on. He did not have a minute to spare, nor a second to waste.

Many, many years before, the angel had heard about the terrible plight of the unhappy earthlings, about how hard and bitter their lives were, and his angel-heart was filled with sympathy. He had fallen, in tears, before the Divine Throne and begged for happiness on behalf of the humans. God accepted his prayer, entrusting the angel with happiness to be delivered to the wretched people of Earth.

Coming down from the seventh Heaven, the angel wandered for many years past suns, stars and comets, in search of the Earth. In his right hand he held happiness and his white wings moved effortlessly through the thin ether. Thousands of years passed; he flew through millions of systems. But no one knew where the Earth with its unhappy people was to be found.

Sometimes a tear fell from the angel's eye. What if his radiant wings were carrying him away from the Earth?

But being an angel, he shed those tears not on account of his own long exile or his endless, futile toil, but for the poor humans who thirsted and strove for the happiness that he carried in his right hand.

"Tell me, please, do you perhaps know where I can find the Earth with its unhappy people?"

"No."

He flew on, driven by his own idealism. Meanwhile the earth grew old and new again. Civilizations, ideologies and religions came and went, but misery continued to reign.

"Where can happiness be found?" sighed the unhappy humans.

Once, an old stargazer, an astronomer, was watching a wandering comet. For a long time he did not take his eye off the lens of his telescope, tracing the comet's every move. He did not abandon his watch. Even when he was eating and sleeping, he would put his young son in his place and as soon as he had finished his meal he would hurry back to resume peering through the lens.

The comet was not pleased:

"What does he want from me, that old wizard? What is the meaning of this? Am I a thief that cannot be left out of one's sight?"

The comet became even angrier.

Suddenly, the angel flew by and asked in his soft, sad voice: "Tell me please, Reb Comet, do you happen to know where I can find the Earth with its unhappy people?"

"People, on the Earth?" answered the comet angrily, "there are only wizards and young thugs there . . ."

"Oh! those poor people," sighed the angel, "all because of unhappiness! No, Reb Comet, you cannot get angry, it is a sin to hate."

And the happiness in his right hand shone and sparkled so brightly that even the comet's mood was lifted when he saw it, and his gloomy, misanthropic soul felt lighter.

"Where is the Earth?"

The comet showed him, pointing with a long, thick beam towards the place where the earth was to be found.

"Oh, how far from heaven the Earth has wandered!" sighed the angel to himself, "and all because of unhappiness."

He immediately set off on his way again.

Meanwhile, on Earth, the astronomer had noticed the angel, spotting, through his telescope, the radiant object in his right hand. And because there was a prophet who had long predicted that an angel would come to deliver happiness, the stargazer immediately recognized that it was the angel come to bring happiness to the people of earth.

The newspapers soon spread the news throughout the whole world.

"An angel is flying our way with happiness," they said, wherever there were people to talk about it.

All the stargazers adjusted their telescopes and saw clearly how the angel was coming closer and closer towards the earth. They began to calculate, and estimated that the angel would land on a specific day, hour, and minute at specific coordinates.

When the day finally came, people from every country gathered at the preordained spot. The place was crowded; people started pushing and shoving one another, getting into arguments. Punches were thrown. It soon came to the point where they started killing each other with knives. Rivers of human blood flowed there, and the wailing and moaning of the dying reached up to the heavens.

The angel saw from afar how the people pushed and crushed each other, and from on high he began to scream with the last of his energy:

"Don't fight! I have enough happiness for everybody, for everybody!"

But they did not hear.

As the angel got closer to the earth, his bright eyes saw the stabbed corpses and the pools of blood, and when his ears heard the wailing and moaning, a tear fell from his glowing eye, landing on the happiness.

From that moment on the happiness was stained.

The crowd watched as the angel—who was tired and weary from his long journey, and from what his eyes had witnessed on Earth—fainted, and the happiness tumbled from his right hand.

1900

SPRING NIGHT

I

The hour was late on an April evening, and a group of young people had gathered in a café.

Springtime in Paris.

Three men formed the basis of this little company: the first, an up-and-coming painter by the name of Baldagin, who had recently gained notoriety; the second, an art critic; the third, a simple connoisseur of art, artists, and amusing gatherings of all kinds. They were joined by a couple of young women, roused by the spring. Ardent living roses fluttered on their bosoms, the scent mingling with the aroma of their perfumes.

The first glasses of champagne had already been drained and, in the high spirits provoked by the vivid odors and the sparkling wine, the conversation turned to the young artist and his new found success.

His rise had been as meteoric as it was unexpected. Suddenly Baldagin was famous, his name on everyone's lips. The art critic, who had always supported and promoted Baldagin throughout his years languishing in obscurity, felt as proud as the artist himself. The whole group saw fit to honor the artist as though he were a young god.

The young women were besotted—in spring, in youth, in fame. So perfect was the atmosphere one could have beckoned spring itself and invited it to join their table.

But after a second glass of champagne the young artist furrowed his arched brow—giving rise to a formation of pronounced ridges—and a mild melancholy washed over his eyes.

"Tell me, Wanda," he said, turning to the young woman beside him, "why does it always feel like there's a worm gnawing at my heart? What do I lack to make me happy?" As he asked this he gently stroked her hair.

She gazed into his eyes with great affection, so charmed that she could not respond.

He continued:

"The world lies before me, mine for the taking. The world has all but conspired to make me happy and yet I torment myself, I am my own worst enemy. I'm plagued by a guilty conscience. Where is the satisfaction, Wanda? Where is the happiness?"

The young artist's lament was greeted with near breathless admiration.

"That's how it must be, you say? All great men must suffer? My friends, do not mistake my words for vain posturing. It wasn't true when I said I was my own worst enemy: I have another enemy, someone who will never create anything true—a colleague of mine by the name of Biros. He came to my exhibition this evening and you should have seen the look of embittered tedium on his face! He looked me over from head to toe, smiling as if to say: so this is how low a person can sink? 'Well now, business is booming,' he said, and those were the only words I heard from him all evening. Business is booming? Imagine!"

Baldagin pounded his fist on the table. "He didn't even *look* properly—there were several pieces he didn't so much as deign to glance at—and then he was gone, that hairy devil . . ."

Wanda could no longer restrain herself; she wrapped her soft arms around his neck and said:

"Oh, my darling, don't think anything of it. He's jealous of you, that good for nothing scoundrel. Forget about him! You've got your health and friends who love you."

The others voiced a chorus of agreement.

"I know full well that he's a good for nothing, but whether he is a scoundrel, or whether he is jealous of me, that I can't be sure of. Either way, his smirk roused my own guilty conscience from its hiding place. It felt as though my conscience had met with its own embodiment, and that they had shaken hands. My guilty conscience has now manifested in a form as hirsute and blond-haired as Biros himself. My conscience has acquired a badly-shaven chin with spiky blond bristles. And it stares at me with a gaze of polished steel. Damn that no good Biros to hell! Wanda, do you know who his lover is? Do you know who he shares a room with? With a *negress*, an ugly thing with rotten teeth, haha!"

He laughed bitterly.

The art critic and aficionados were curious about this swarthy character with the blond stubbly chin and his negress. They bombarded the artist with questions: Who was this Biros? What kind of art did he make? Where did he come from?

"Leave me in peace!" Baldagin growled. "Here, take his address and go up to visit him yourself. He can hold his own with you critics and connoisseurs—chattering and babbling endlessly about art. I loathe him, despise him from the very pit of my heart, just as I despise my guilty conscience."

"And yet you live with your conscience and will never free yourself of it," the critic interjected.

The women demanded more champagne and pressed Baldagin for details about Biros' black lover: Does her body shine like a polished shoe? Can she dance? Does she eat mice?

Their curiosity mounted until finally, at around one in the morning, it was decided that there was no option but to pay Biros a visit.

A dispirited Baldagin followed them. Provisions of champagne and liqueurs were packed on the off chance they might be required.

In the meantime spring had retreated from the Parisian streets. A damp wind started to blow. The ladies were obliged to hold on to their hats tightly, and the wind filled the capes of the gentlemen like sails.

II

The members of the little fellowship were breathless, their hearts trembling with fatigue, by the time they reached the seventh-floor artist's atelier of "Biros the Hirsute." The sombre glow of a kerosene lamp, positioned in a corner, was the atelier's sole source of light. One could barely see a short distance in front of one's nose. The visitors were constantly bumping into various objects, and there were many things to be startled by.

One visitor stumbled onto the sleeping place of Biros's lover who was lying on the couch wearing nothing but a blouse. He sprang up as though from a hot stove as he spied in the darkness a glint of light reflected in her eyes. He was so stunned he almost screamed. A second person found himself standing face to face with an enormous goat's head—a clay sculpture—and he could have sworn he saw the ears move. Had it not just jiggled its beard at him? A third stood before another beast—a pig, or perhaps a tiger, eyes bulging in stiff-necked silence . . . But the most frightening of all was the short, blond-haired man—Biros himself. He was standing in his suspenders, his grubby shirt wide open. One could see that his arms were muscular, his shoulders broad, and his legs short. From his tangled mane of blond hair protruded a large forehead framing a pair of beady, squinting eyes. There was something bullish about his hoarse voice.

"A bit late for a visit," he said, still unable to conceal his surprise.

Baldagin introduced him, one by one, to his acquaintances in a round of wordless handshakes.

"Listen, Biros, you blond devil, I have come to pay you a visit. I want my drunk companions to have a look at you, along with your famous goat and pig heads. That fellow there is an art critic. And this is Wanda who knows more about art than all the experts put together."

Wanda approached him and looked him over with the clear, flattering gaze of her eyes, which shared the same softness as her skin.

"So you're the harsh critic? Let me have a look at you, guilty conscience!"

Biros flashed her a smile, revealing his black, unbrushed teeth.

"I'm no critic. I have no interest in any of that. I make my art the way I feel it. It flows from me and flows back into me. I am both the creator and admirer of my works. Beyond that I don't know. No one knows about me either. I don't criticize. I don't care a fig for the business of art criticism. It's a marketplace."

"Come now, Biros," said Baldagin, "we'll listen to your insinuations another time. Now we want to drink. You used to have a taste for good cognac if I remember correctly?"

But Wanda protested:

"Let him speak."

With the keen instincts of a woman she discerned a wholeness, an unbrokenness in the severe manner of his speech. Biros's little eyes sparkled and he smiled his best smile for her, opening his mouth wide and letting out a barely discernible raspy laugh.

He had taken a liking to her.

For Wanda's benefit he became talkative, more animated, and they emptied one bottle after another.

The negress was compelled to drink her portion alone in the confines of her couch, for when she had attempted to rise and get dressed Biros shoved her back down—an instruction to stay where she was.

They laughed, made mischief, and joked with the Negress. They sat down beside her on her couch. She sang, half seated, a Portuguese song which she'd brought with her from her native land of Brazil. It was a sad, toneless song, and it melted into the darkness through which only silhouettes could be seen, and the looming heads of strange beasts: the heads of dogs, cows, goats and all manner of fantastic horned creatures, with jaws either wired shut or gaping wide with protruding tongues.

Baldagin lay slumped in a corner by himself, drunk and dejected, staring at the goat's head illuminated in the lamplight.

Only Wanda paid any attention to Biros, staying close to him the whole time. The allure of her body had gone to his head like a sweet fog, and she teased out his most intimate thoughts, as a seasoned fisherman maneuvers the rod out of muddy waters:

"Art should be mute," he labored to speak for her. "*His* kind talk too much," he said, gesturing toward Baldagin. "He speaks, makes a racket, makes himself seen—it is a poor imitation of what real life is. What use is art to us? They have a better understanding of it out on the boulevards. Art should be absolute, all encompassing. We should kneel down before it and pray—Anything less is meaningless . . .

"In everything there is some eternity, some stillness and silence. Whoever sees it sees it, whoever doesn't see it does not and never will see it . . ."

Wanda settled her hands on his arms and he went on.

"They speak of some higher pleasure that art can give? But one woman can give more pleasure than all the world's artists combined. But women are not art, and art is not pleasure. Pleasure is psychology, movement—do you understand what I'm saying?—ephemerality. Art must be all encompassing, like death, like eternity . . ."

One by one the others came closer and began to listen. Only Baldagin remained at a distance. An old clock ticked, striking three like a hiccough.

"Wanda, come here," came his voice from the corner.

"You come here to us, Biros is sharing the credo of his art. I want to hear, join us!"

"Come here I said, I'm afraid . . . this goat's head here—I'm going to destroy it . . ."

Wanda went to him, leading Biros with her by the hand.

All three stood around the goat's head, staring at it for some time. Wanda dropped to her knees and covered her face with her hands as though in prayer. She looked to Biros as if seeking his approval.

He took her by the hands and lifted her to her feet.

More wine and liqueur was consumed.

And as the clock struck four Biros, drunk and inflamed, pounded the plinths on which his sculptures stood with his fist and bellowed that Wanda must strip naked in front of him.

"You have undressed my soul, I've exposed everything to you: now you must show me your body!"

The Negress sprang up from her couch wearing nothing but a blouse and when she heard what was happening she pulled off the blouse and began to dance in a frenetic rhythm.

There was nothing else for it, Biros insisted, and the other women had no choice but to strip naked too.

The gray light of dawn began to appear through the windows. They extinguished the lamp.

Baldagin was still lying in the corner, screaming that the goat head had eaten its way into his soul, that it was consuming him . . .

Wanda dragged him forcefully out of his corner and the whole company danced in a circle around the goat head.

Wanda sang:

> *Goat head! Goat head!*
> *Hop Hop! Hop!*
> *Eternity, eternity, swallow us up!*

Biros quietly broke away from the circle and stepped aside. He rested his chin in his hands and his beady eyes smiled gaily.

When Baldagin saw this he experienced a terrible rage. With all his strength he struck the plinth, smashing the goat's head to pieces.

He screamed as if in a nightmare: "It is my guilty conscience. I have destroyed it! There you have it, you crooked philosopher!"

Biros did not budge.

The women grabbed their clothes and covered their bodies. The early morning light became suddenly bright and stringent.

The great city, visible through the window, began to take on new colors: the gray hues of a working day.

No one dared to speak. No one made eye contact. Only the Negress continued to make noise, leaping in her dusky nudity, until she fell down, unconscious.

Wordlessly, the guests began to take their leave.

1923

WAKING

A bright, frosty winter's night hangs over the sleepy little town. In the dark blue sky the moon is round and pure, its fine, steely light fills the air, enshrouding the small, bent wooden houses. Only the large chimney of the town's sole factory and the high spire of the church breach the heights, casting dark blemishes into the pure air.

The shine from the sky's thousand stars bounces off the frozen snowflakes, shattering into a million shards of light directed back into the heavens. The air is cold, staid and calm, without the slightest movement—all around is still. The little wooden houses bow down toward the ground, sleepy, dreamy, and a pitch darkness peers out of their windows—all except for one, which lets out a weak, flickering light together with a tearful, choking voice: a sick child awakens and cries. Soon the clacking of a rocking crib is heard, and silence once again re-conquers the still, frosty night.

In the tight embrace of the night, the world holds its tongue as though afraid to speak in view of the beautiful, mighty nocturnal queen. Only the insolent clock-tower remains unintimidated, ringing out every quarter hour, issuing a curt, laconic report on the lateness of the hour, and the expected duration of the night's reign over the world.

Bong . . . Bong . . . Bong . . . Bong . . . The clock strikes four. But the night, feigning ignorance of clock-language, behaves as though it will rule for ever, remaining unmoving, serene and majestic.

The townsfolk have long been sleeping a deep, late-night slumber, resting their heavy bones, and weary minds as much as they can: the young lie on broken beds, huddled against each other to warm their cold bodies, while the elderly shiver on their alcove beds over the now cold masonry stoves. In the Jewish houses, the stoves are empty and so there is a mess of entangled arms and legs, pressed together in strange bunks, like goods packed away in a crate; a few pale, childish faces peek out and yarmulkes fall to the floor. And on every face, in the beds and over the masonry stoves, in Jewish and in Christian homes, a kind of satisfaction spreads over everything, and with their noses they play a song of praise to the good, merciful Creator, who granted them such a pleasant night, such sweet slumber.

The small hand of the clock slides onwards from the four, creeping closer to the five. The watchman rises from the stairs of a storehouse, yawns with gaping mouth and heads home to sleep. The peaceful air is disturbed by a cry of *cock-a-doodle-doo.*

Things are on the move. The night shivers in fear of its own demise.

Bong . . . Bong . . . The clock strikes five.

And in that very second a drawling whistle sounds from the factory. The noise spreads through the air, moving far and wide, forcing its way in through the windows and waking:

Psssst . . . Get up, man! Get up for work!

In a few seconds the children will begin to stir in their beds, turning a few times from one side to the other; soon they will yawn and rise.

A young mother, having only just opened her eyes, grabs her baby and stuffs a breast into its mouth: the infant needs to drink enough milk to last until midday when she comes home for lunch. The children wash in haste, placing the bread that has been prepared the previous evening into their pockets.

Outside all is quiet once again; until the church bell begins to move.

It rings out steady and torpid. Soon a second bell rings, at a lower pitch than the first, but faster, and their voices merge in mournful harmony. The ringing carries in the air, stealing in through the windows, waking those inside:

Bong . . . Bong—Bong . . . Bong—Bong—Bong . . . Get up. Get up, human and serve God!

There is stirring in the alcoves above the stoves; the elderly scratch, yawn and rise.

There is movement on the street; human figures come into view: old and young, men and women hurry in two directions—the young towards the factory, and the old towards the church.

The Jewish shops open up, the *shammes* hits his hammer, waking the people for prayer. Craftsmen with *tallis* and *tefillin* under their arms hurry into the prayer house.

Soon thereafter the town's clock strikes seven announcing that soon the sun will make an appearance.

And the sun emerges from behind the low houses, red and fresh, sending bright, energizing beams in every direction, weaving light into the morning air, streaming in through the windows and waking:

Get up, people, get up to serve yourselves! For holy is man!

But the sun finds no one in their beds; they have long been serving others, some their God, and some their masters.

The sun casts a scornful glance at the earth and hides itself away behind a heavy cloud . . .

1916

THE PHILOSOPHER

He is a student of philosophy, residing at the university dormitories, but for two reasons I fear he will not graduate alongside his classmates. First, he's running out of money, and second, try as he might, he just seems incapable of wrapping his head around Kant.

It's pitiful, his friends say, to observe him in the seminarium. He torments himself, the poor fellow, sitting there with a hangdog expression on his face, straining his feeble brain. He has an unshakable admiration for philosophy, and not just the discipline itself, with its narrow definitions and fine-tuned differentiations, which his bookkeeper's head, accustomed to round-numbers, cannot get to the bottom of; in his modesty he also harbors a profound respect toward his professors, his fellow-students, and people in general.

But what brought him to philosophy?

It's difficult to fathom. For ten years he worked as a bookkeeper, starting as an errand-boy and advancing all the way up to a respectable monthly wage. An uncomplicated man, lacking any trace of hollow arrogance, or foolish vanity; a man without fantasies whose only thought was of getting his next raise, or climbing one rung higher up the ladder—just imagine a fellow like that becoming a philosopher: contemplating the problems of the world, pondering mortality, the meaning of life, and all that.

Admittedly, the aforementioned questions have a tendency to show up unbidden, as likely to come knocking on the door of the lowliest water-carrier, as that of a cultivated man. But who pays them such heed? A thought flashes through one's mind one minute and is gone the next. But to throw away a livelihood and to drop everything and set off for Zurich to study philosophy?—Now that's truly a rarity!

Yet that's exactly what happened to this fellow. He had attained the highest and best position in his field, beyond which one simply cannot rise in his profession. He became chief accountant with a salary of a hundred and thirty rubles a month and that's when he suddenly became aware of an emptiness. His ambitions ceased and he came to a standstill, feeling that his life no longer held any meaning.

His mind was accustomed to feeding off hope and fantasies about advancing his career. But when the cog was removed from the machinery he was left helpless, no longer knowing what to do with himself.

And it happened that while he was writing, eating, or walking, he would find himself mulling over an idea of truly philosophical import: What was the purpose of it all? Why must he die one day? What did he really want to live for?

Naturally his impoverished brain could find no answers to these questions.

By day the situation was still tolerable. At night, however, when he found himself lying in bed all alone the thoughts would arrive like black, gloomy shadows and would refuse to leave. And because he had a natural inclination to melancholia, he was beset by a terrible fear: the fear of madness.

Once he went to seek the advice of a famous Yiddish writer, that is to say, to ask him in his capacity as a "man of some renown" to answer the questions that plagued him.

He entered, and spoke very self-consciously, but the writer could not understand what he was trying to communicate.

"Don't take it the wrong way that I've come to ask you something," he said nervously, and his face radiated so much suffering that the writer's interest was piqued. "I wanted to ask you about . . . I wanted you to explain the whole business of life, you understand?"

The writer regarded him with a wise, benevolent expression, and invited him to take off his coat, and have a seat so that they could discuss the matter at leisure.

"You want me to answer *all* the questions of philosophy?" the writer asked with a smile "What can I say? Each person must find his own answers to those questions. Have you studied philosophy?"

"I have never found the time," the accountant explained. Taking leave of the writer, he determined that he had no choice but to study philosophy. He was convinced that the heavy tomes of contemporary and ancient philosophy must contain the answers, the true answers to all the questions that plagued him, one only had to make the effort, and work diligently. His experience as an accountant led him to the conviction that with enough hard work, effort, and consistency, there was nothing in this world that one could not achieve.

Through thrift and austere living he had saved a few hundred rubles, enough to live on for several years.

One morning he bid farewell to his employer, paid a final visit to the famous writer, and then set off to study philosophy abroad.

Years passed. For two long years he wore himself out preparing for the university entrance examination. During that time his questions about the world became less pressing, and his fear of losing his mind faded. For the time being the machinery of his brain had regained it's missing component: ambition, the desire to pass the entrance exam. And so he happily ate his meagre meals, slept well, and studied with great diligence.

When he was accepted into university he once again experienced a moment of elation, a joy that reminded him of the times his boss had given him a promotion.

By now he has been learning for several years, but without great success. He feels that the books and professors are leading him around in circles, without even getting close to the heart of the matter, the meaning of life itself.

Sometimes the practical bookkeeper's instinct awakens inside him, and he feels that this whole branch of inquiry is superficial, based on appearances, lacking a solid foundation.

And yet he has respect for philosophy, not because he has such great confidence in its ability to answer his thorny questions, but because it is so deep, so difficult for his mind to penetrate, because he must struggle to grasp the true meaning, the correct significance of each new philosophical term.

His money, though, is running out and his hair is beginning to turn gray. He intends to return to Warsaw, to try to return to working as an accountant.

I have my doubts that he will be able to find a position like the one he had before. But no matter; he is prepared to take a position for only forty rubles a month for the time being—he is prepared to start again from the beginning.

No matter!—with hard work and determination there's nothing one can't achieve in this world.

1911

SHE AND I

Sit yourself down, angelic child.

How beautiful you are, sitting peacefully—your head leaning on your right hand, the left held before your mouth, drumming your fingertips against your young, fresh lips. Sit like that and contemplate the sky with your clear, pious, believing eyes.

The window is high. You sit near it, where your eyes can see half the heavens and count the stars as they crawl, one after another, ashamed and pensive, out from under the glaucous sky.

Darkness shrouds the earth, the buildings merge as one. Even the pump in the centre of the market square loses itself in the murky fog and appears now like an inkblot on a sheet of gray paper . . . Only those in the background—those bent, familiar people—still stir amid the tranquil, silent darkness . . .

What is there to see in this unlit world?

Your eyes behold half the heavens. Look, and your pure, childish thoughts will take shape undisturbed. Let them flow, like a slow river over a sandy bed. And cursed be any stone that blocks their sacred path!

My child! Am I not cursing myself? Am I, too, not a stone, which disturbs you, which blocks your coursing thoughts?

Woe to him whose life has made him bent, woe to him!

Does my presence here in this room disturb you? Are your thoughts not diverted from their rightful path when my image assaults your eyes? Do you not feel my searching gaze wander over your face? Your hand twitched suddenly just now, brushing the hair from your brow: was that not old anger building in your heart against me; the protest of childhood against a grown, bent man who does not allow you to be childish?

But now night is falling. The sky grows darker, the stars brighter. Here is the moon, emerging from behind the rooftops across the way, spreading its soft, pale beams all around . . . Pay attention, my child, and give your soul over to the wide, unknowing sky; may your thoughts be born one after another and fly away from you with fond farewells like doves from a dovecote.

Think. Think my child!

. . . *now I'm thirteen years old . . . another two years and I'll have a fiancé . . . with ruddy cheeks, black, curly sidelocks, a black gabardine, a velvet hat, shy and pensive, with downcast eyes . . .*

"It is good to be a bride . . . mazl tov," they'll say to me. I'll braid my hair at the back, and comb my hair at the front . . . I'll put on a hat and go for a walk, as if nothing has happened . . .

"The groom will be invited over, but I won't look at him, on no account, I'll storm out into the next room . . .

Afterward—a wedding, they dance while I sit there in my white silk dress . . .

. . . I lie in bed, I am with child, Mother-in-law comes in to wish me mazl tov, I do not answer—I am weak . . .

Afterward—I marry off my own children, I am now a mother-in-law . . . a grandmother . . .

My child! Why have you suddenly risen to your feet? What is the meaning behind the mourning I see upon your face? Aha! You have remembered your grandmother's death all those years ago! You remembered that they dressed her in white shrouds and carried her out of the house in order to hide her away in the ground!

Was it Death that passed through your thoughts? Was that the clap of his dark wings in your young mind?

Oh! Curse him too, that Death!

The room is now dark. By the window you hide your face in your hands, and I hear a sigh, a sigh from deep within your heart, sweet child.

Come here, closer to me, come! Why won't you look me in the eye?

Come here and we'll play: clap your small hands against mine . . . one, two, three . . .

Now you have raised your eyes, our glances meet— you snatch your hand away from mine, and run away, and now I am alone. My shadow and I; the lamp glows dimly, the shadow seems to speak to me, or I to it:

Woe to you, grown man, woe! How could childhood tolerate you? How could a child's eyes look upon your face, a face over which life has dragged its plows, leaving behind such deep, long furrows?

112

Come my child, have pity! Here I have filled a whole sheet of paper thinking about you; take it, my child, crumple it up, make a paper trumpet and cry out, loud and cheerful, in childlike freedom: "cock-a-doo-dle-doo!" and I will rest assured that the paper has not gone to waste.

For . . . who has ever heard of a yearning that could regain a childhood gone by?

1902

A VICTIM OF INGRATITUDE

Gelerman arrived in Warsaw toward the beginning of the Haskalah-era in Poland. Something was rumbling in the provinces: It seemed that every few days a new town was shaken by the news of another yeshiva boy who had abandoned it all—Talmud, synagogue, his parents, and sometimes even a bride—and set off to study worldly matters. In those days there was an organization in Warsaw that supported these newcomers, providing them with a new wardrobe of European-style short jackets, Polish lessons and the like. The most promising boys—or at least those most skilled at knocking on doors, who knew how best to please potential benefactors—often received financial aid, and were sent abroad to study modern theology at Western universities.

But Gelerman was not one of those skilled at knocking on doors, nor at pleasing potential benefactors. And so, six months after arriving in Warsaw, he had been left to fend for himself. He found work in a shop, being paid initially only in room and board and later with an additional two rubles a week.

For Gelerman this outcome was satisfactory. He dreamed of distant horizons, which he had pictured in his imagination even before he had left his village, but he considered these musings as a temporary salve, just something to get him through the day, a way to rest a little after a hard day elbowing his way through the streets, climbing countless flights of stairs, and ringing countless doorbells. He believed that tomorrow, or the next day, he would finally cast off his hardship and make a start toward his true destiny, the reason he had come to the city in the first place. And so a year passed, followed by another, and the hope in his heart took on ever more fanciful forms.

During that time Gelerman received a letter from an acquaintance back home. As usual the letter spoke of Haskalah, of enlightenment, of the obscurity that reigned within the Tents of Jacob, etc. That same letter mentioned a boy by the name of Shmaye-Getsl, who was in a wretched state, with nothing to eat and barely a stitch on his back; there was no question of his studying as he had neither a place to go, nor books. The story of Shmaye-Getsl stayed with Gelerman: such a desperate predicament it was. He pictured the boy's browbeaten face, the downcast eyes which only looked up in order to communicate that he was hungry, or cold, hoping to inspire pity.

That is when Gelerman had the idea of bringing Shmaye-Getsl to Warsaw to make something of him. The thought that such a slovenly, despondent, helpless creature could complete a doctorate, or perhaps be transformed into a *rabbiner,*[1] so enchanted Gelerman that he wasted no time in writing to his acquaintance to tell Shmaye-Getsl to come to Warsaw. But Shmaye-Getsl arrived in a frightful state: dressed in rags, barefoot, his hat falling apart. Gelerman who was waiting to meet him at the train station was startled when he saw him, but in his mind he pictured Shmaye-Getsl's future: elegantly dressed, educated and westernized, and as was his habit in such moments he felt exhilarated and confident. He signalled for a carriage—he was too ashamed to be seen walking with Shmaye-Getsl—and took him home. By the next morning Shmaye-Getsl was well-fed, dressed in decent clothes, and ready to begin his studies.

Shaye-Getsl, it turned out, was quite a passive individual, seemingly without a will of his own. He barely spoke. If someone sent him to a lesson, he went. If not, he sat at home and learned there. He did not even get dressed unless someone suggested he should. All in all he had the base nature of a beggar, but with the energy, patience, and work-ethic of a healthy, if somewhat limited, character.

During the next two years Shmaye-Getsl lived at Gelerman's expense. He made progress, studying in Dikshteyn's school which had a good reputation all over Poland. Gradually Shmaye-Getsl learned how to knock on the right doors. His pitiful face seemed ideally suited to helping him find his way in the world. He received alms and soon thereafter he was sent abroad with a scholarship donated by a wealthy man.

---

1 A non-orthodox rabbi.

Bidding him farewell, Gelerman beamed with pride, and said:

"You'll see, Shmaye-Getsl, you'll be ashamed of me yet..."

And Shmaye-Getsl hung his head, while mumbling in a pleading, almost tearful voice:

"You are my savior; what would I have done without you? You have saved me..."

Years passed and Gelerman found himself ever more tightly strapped into life's yoke; he was earning more but also consuming more. In time he also married, had children, and became widowed. Life, in all its tyranny, hastened ever onwards, turning Gelerman into a tiny cog, spinning along in the whirr of the surrounding machinery, running and racing without a will of its own, without recourse to pleasure. By nature a calm, pensive man, Gelerman had become melancholic, without cheer or enjoyment from life. In his heart his old hopes had never been extinguished, hopes for enlightenment, dreams of the free, honest life he had once imagined for himself. Nothing had come of all that, and existence was now a struggle, only getting harder with each passing day. Life held no purpose, never allowing pause for a moment of joy. The days and years dragged on in endless succession bringing nothing but worries, stress and drudgery.

And here, in the toughest, saddest moment of his life, when he had tired of everything, in his heart a tiny, happy voice piped up: He remembered Shmaye-Getsl who had studied at a university abroad, who was already preparing to return to Poland as a doctor, and experienced an unfamiliar feeling of relief. He had not lived in vain; he had indeed done some good in the world.

On occasion Gelerman would be visited by guests, acquaintances he neither loved nor actively disliked. They played cards, filling the whole room with cigarette smoke. His children would wake up, and the guests would linger until well into the night. Sometimes they drank beer or spirits. Gelerman, impressionable by nature, would soon get excited. Intoxicated, his eyes began to sparkle, and in a hoarse voice he cried out:

"What do I need all this for! Did you know that Shmaye-Getsl has finished his doctorate now? I swear it as I live and breathe! A doctor! The very same Shmaye-Getsl I brought here in rags."

Lately he had not received any letters from Shmaye-Getsl. But he did not feel any resentment about the lack of correspondence. It was no trifle, passing exams to become a doctor! No doubt Shmaye-Getsl was busy, with no time to spare. But when he comes back to Warsaw, just think of the welcome he'll receive! Imagine having a dear friend of such stature, a doctor! And Gelerman began to count the weeks until the end of the summer when his friend—who was now known as Dr. Barger—would come, and he felt an unforeseen energy within himself; fresh hope began to grow in his heart.

From that day on Gelerman could think of almost nothing else. What would Shmaye-Getsl look like now?

He daydreamed about their meeting, about sitting to-gether and catching up. These thoughts monopolized his inner world and he grew impatient for the happy day to arrive . . .

✳

What had happened? Was the world not the same one Gelerman knew? Or had there been some terrible mix up in his mind and he had misunderstood everything.

He knew that Dr. Barger was in Warsaw. He knew he had paid visits to all the wealthy patrons who had supported him. He even knew where he lived, and that he had immediately found a job as a mechanical engineer with a salary of a hundred and fifty rubles a month. He had made some inquiries and found out about everything. Everything: where he ate, where he spent the day, which Synagogue he went to on Shabbes, how he went around coiffed and clean-shaven. And yet he understood absolutely nothing.

What had happened?

The truth of the matter is that nothing had hap-pened. Dr. Barger had simply forgotten all about his erstwhile benefactor. And when an acquaintance who happened to know about his connection to Gelerman reminded him of it, Dr. Barger turned pale at first, tugged at his mustache and then said in Polish:

"Oh yes, I knew him once . . . Now, what was it we were talking about?"

He was ashamed, or perhaps afraid to meet Gelerman. He was striving to be accepted at the wealthy salons; that was now his sole mission in life and anything that could jeopardize his chances was to be avoided like the plague.

What happened next was an entirely routine affair, but Gelerman was unable to comprehend it. A strange confusion reigned in his mind, everything had turned topsy-turvy and he could no longer understand, nor trust his senses. His melancholy intensified, plaguing him by day, keeping him awake at night. He forgot how things stood.

Trudging through the streets one dreary autumn day Gelerman spotted, from afar, a man with a top hat on his finely groomed young head walking toward him. As he drew nearer he recognized the man as Shmaye-Getsl. His pitiful face, peeking out from under the top hat, was the same as always. Gelerman held his breath. He could barely move his legs. What would happen?

Dr. Barger glanced at him—a strange unsure glance. He turned pale: there could be no doubt that he had recognized Gelerman, but he soon composed himself, motioned with his cane and turning his face to the side, he walked right past.

Gelerman was frozen to the spot. He felt a violent twinge in his chest before falling to the ground. Afterwards he had no more thoughts, and no more memories.

1928

AT THE BALL

Why are you so ugly?

You came all dressed up for the ball. The velvet, satin, and silk let out a cry: "You have contaminated us with your ugliness. You have killed our splendor with the dull gaze of your eyes."

Why are you so ugly?

Piano tones trickle down from the stage and a sweet singer loses himself in Tchaikovsky's romance, a spring evening pours down from the stage, a thousand future generations sobbing in unison . . . The girl closes her eyes, opens her blossoming lips and offers herself up as a sacrifice—the magic of generations to come.

And well-fed men sit, broader than the chairs on which their bodies rest.

One of them yawns.

A second gazes into space.

A third looks down at his polished shoes.

While a fourth is suddenly concerned about his money: "Anna, did you remember to lock the bedroom door?"

※

Why are you so ugly?

When you came into this world you were more beautiful than a flower. The million generations that came before you blessed your birth. A cool dew lay upon your childhood: a clever, young creature grew up, with eyes trained on the heavens—mankind.

Where has God's blessing gone? The life and the love that brought you into this world—where are they?

I contemplated for a moment: they are spring-powered mechanisms, wound up to last seventy-years.

Nature created a duration, a playtime for its beloved children, for those who live life for the sake of laughter and fun.

But their breath was poisoned, a deathly savagery lay over their faces. And they screamed with gaping mouths:

"We are the lords of the world!"

And as proof they proffered all the money, and every diamond on this earth.

※

What shall I do with my disgust for you? Where can I dispose of the shame of my own life?

If you are life;
If humanity consists of those like you and I?
How is one to tolerate sharing a world with you?

Why are you so ugly?

1920

THE SINFUL WORLD

During a period of solitude I lay alone in my room. There was no bread in the house, the roads were burdened with snow, and there was no transportation—a haunting feeling. It was cold and dark in the room—the gas and electricity had gone out and in a dismal slumber I tossed and turned from one side to another. My nerves were pulled taut, like the cord of a bow: from fear of pogroms, from the thought that an entire people is condemned to live like dogs . . . the slightest noise from the yard sounded, to my senses, like a thunderclap, the slightest rattle of the panes resounded with deafening intensity as though the earth itself were shaking from a cataclysm, and buildings were collapsing all around me. Every sound coming from outside was duplicated and magnified many times over. The weak, tired circulation of the blood to my eyes throbbed in my temples like the rhythmic hacking of woodsmen: one, two—one, two—one, two . . .

"Well, why? Why?" my heart wept. "Why all this suffering without end? The war is over; why does the world not return to peace?"

With that thought I fell asleep and stopped count-ing the hammer-blows of blood in my temples.

Someone woke me, told me to get up. His voice was callous and severe. I knew: my life was at stake.

1920

FRIENDSHIP

I

Yes, it was jealousy, pure and simple. He had caught himself red-handed: his feelings were no mystery to him.

His friend, his closest friend, perhaps even his only friend, with whom he had shared years of loneliness, had become abhorrent to him. He could no longer look him in the eye, could no longer exchange a few simple words with him. His face had grown repulsive; his every expression, his every smirk, irritated and exasperated him. His friend's gentle smile, the same smile he had once loved so well, now seemed false, hollow and unbearable; his sharp, pithy words were now as meaningless as those of a parrot.

It was almost a year since his wedding and he loved his wife more with each passing day. He—the perennial loner on the wrong side of thirty—could scarcely have believed that the love of a single woman could bring him such deep happiness, could transform gloomy days into bright, heady celebrations, intoxicating him daily with fresh joys, with new, untested, unimagined blessings.

It had been a fortuitous choice, proving him to be a man of taste. Etta's beauty did not glow or shine or call attention to itself. She dressed and acted so modestly, so unassumingly, that at first glance she hardly made an impression at all. But now he knew that she hid her beauty, keeping it just for the man she had chosen. The graceful contours of her body, her fine, elegant neck, her soft, shapely arms, which seemed to have been built for embracing—even these were mysteries for him to uncover gradually: a book full of poetry and splendor, to be leafed through, revealing new delights on each page.

He was happy. His business affairs, which he had been running himself for three years now, were going well; his clouded eyes had grown clear, his mood was lighter and fresher. He experienced a second youth.

Happy people experience a desire to see their friends happy; those who are happily married acquire the tendency to arrange matches for their friends. This feeling is what prompted him to seek out his old friend, a Yiddish poet, and invite him to stay with them. God knows his intention was not to boast, or vaunt his happiness. Deep down he hoped his friend would finally set aside his dreams and become a practical man. Perhaps if he saw for himself he would want to get married and experience the same happiness.

Like his friend, he too had once dabbled in literature, had gone hungry, had been constantly lonely and bitter, had philosophized endlessly about life, while life for its part had cast him aside into a dark corner. But in the end he had come to his senses and now he was happy.

In the quiet, pleasant moments of domestic contentment, when he and Etta would sit by the table after dinner, as the lamp burned brightly, and the sounds of the street would carry into the room like a rhythmic expression of life, he liked to stroke Etta's light-colored hair, seeking out her little ear and softly, slowly, kissing it. In those moments he would tell her stories about his former life and about his friend. He described his friend as a deeply intellectual man, recounting anecdotes about his bohemian lifestyle, and to his great joy he noticed that Etta had sympathy for such a fellow, and took an interest in him.

In addition to the beauty of his dear wife's body, each day he also discovered new facets to her soul, ever more refinement and noble intellect. That girl, whom he'd snatched away from a dressmaker's, had a feel for the finer things; she understood people, and using her feminine instinct she could size them up remarkably well. She was no stranger to the workings of the human mind.

And so one evening before bed he read to her from his friend's poems, and certain passages brought tears to Etta's eyes. He was grateful to his friend who had unwittingly helped him to explore the depths of Etta's feelings.

"Why doesn't he come visit us?" she asked.

She had met him once. Shortly after their wedding he had come to pay his respects and had stayed no more than half an hour. He had never shown himself since.

"He is a wild man. He has no love for quiet houses. He can abide either the bustling throngs of the streets, the great masses, or his own solitude, but nothing in between. You know, Etta," he added with a smile, "we are petit-bourgeois, and he is a poet, after all. Our place is so fussy . . . so middle-class and so proper."

He kissed her, and she rested her bare, delicate arms on his shoulders.

"My dear . . ." She sat on his lap, and continued talking about his friend.

"The poets have a different sort of life," she said. "They fly so very far away and they think so differently. I would be afraid to live with a poet, he has such a strange gaze."

"You think his gaze is frightening? No, he is a good-hearted man."

"No, I know, he has kind eyes. But when he looked at me, I felt so uneasy. He stares the way chickens stare sometimes, or dogs."

"Chickens or dogs? That's how you see him? You mean little thing you." And he kissed her again on the lips.

"Stop it—you don't understand," and she slapped his hand. "I mean his gaze is so alien, so distant, there's something quite different about it."

He looked at her with wonder and joy. How well she expressed it, how correctly she had described the gaze of his old friend.

The next time he met his friend he invited him to their home, and from that day on he became a regular visitor.

That is also when it all began.

The jealousy crept in, subtly and unnoticed into his heart, and like a disease which one carries unknowingly inside, it grew until it was ripe.

II

Etta was asleep in her bed; the room was dark. Midnight had long since passed. Her husband tossed and turned, unable to sleep. This was his first sleepless night, marking the end of his happy days.

What exactly had he noticed? Nothing; it was nothing at all. His friend was now a regular visitor—What of it? After all, he had invited him to visit many times, and he was a lonely man, and Etta was interesting and beautiful. Yet somehow his friend's eyes, those chicken-like, dog-like eyes, had acquired an unusual sheen . . . Was it not foolish, petty even, to be suspicious of a shine in someone's eyes, and to poison one's own life because of it? Certainly it was—foolish and petty. What else? When he caressed Etta, a smile played across her lips that he did not understand. Again: foolishness. She had become a woman, her girlish naivety had vanished like a lifting fog, it was the smile of a ripe woman, an Eve who had sated her curiosity by eating the forbidden fruit . . . Just this evening, two hours ago, when she became sleepy and tired, he felt such strong love for her that he embraced her and kissed her passionately, to the point of oblivion. And suddenly he saw the smile on her lips—a new smile—and it opened his eyes.

Now he knew the true meaning of her smiling eyes. It was a new beauty which he had discovered in his Etta. He had known her so superficially up to that point. Every day brought something new. Oh, what an idiot he was, how petty! To have such suspicions, to cast such aspersions on his one and only dear Etta like that!

As for the time she brushed her fingers against his friend's hand, that had been an accident; she was handing him some tea and wanted to pass him the sugar at the same time, an accident! . . .

His nerves were just on edge, that was all: on account of that contested promissory note he'd received that morning . . . he could hear the whistle of a train, somehow he thought he could even hear the sound of the wheels—he had no idea the railway was so close . . . Etta was asleep, uneasily it seemed; sometimes he heard her breathing, and sometimes it stopped abruptly . . .

He said her name quietly, barely a whisper:

"Etta . . ."

And she answered:

"You're not asleep? What is it, Khayim?"

"It's Nothing. I was asleep, but I had a strange dream, that's all. What time is it?"

"It's gone two o'clock."

"Two o'clock? You know, I'm not sure if I turned the lamp off properly."

The story with the lamp was pure invention; He wanted to see Etta's face, to read something from it.

He lit the lamp and approached her bed. She lay snuggled up in the blanket and pillows. As he approached she turned her head toward him, her face entirely obscured by her voluminous hair. He brushed the hair from her face, and he felt as though he did so not with the hand of a lover, but with the cold hand of an inquisitor and judge. He wanted to see her face. She looked a little tired, and so very beautiful . . . but her face betrayed no hint of what he wanted to know.

"Do you love me, Etta?"

She opened her eyes and looked at him.

God! Was that not the same far-away stare—like that of a chicken or a dog—that she had once discerned in his friend's gaze? And how was he to interpret her cold smile?

With a tragic tone in his voice, a crack audible even to himself, he asked her again:

"Do you love me, Etta!"

"You really need to know that at two o'clock in the morning? Go back to sleep, my love."

She caressed his head. Obeying her like a child he put out the lamp and went back to bed.

"My love," that's what she'd said. He repeated the word a hundred times in his mind.

"Love . . ." But *how* had she said it? What lay within? Was she trying to console him, as one consoles a foolish little boy? "My love" and not "my dear"? Why not "dear"?—this was foolishness! But why was she not asleep? What was keeping her awake?

At worst the only explanation could be that she was in love with his friend, but nothing had happened. But if there were nothing, her sleep would not be disturbed; that much was clear. He had a busy day ahead of him, and as misfortune would have it he could not get to sleep.

The clock struck three, then four, and all the while his anxiety rose. His body was entirely bathed in sweat, his temples throbbed.

"Etta," he called out softly, with a pleading exasperation in his tone, but no voice answered him from the other bed; Etta's breathing had become even and regular. She was asleep.

An oppressive dread and terror befell him. How was it all going to end? What would happen? Jealousy— That's what it was. And this was just the beginning; there was so much more to come . . . clouded days, sleepless nights . . .

He would pay dearly for those few months of happiness. Indeed, nothing comes for free in this world. What had he done to earn a second youth? This was how he would pay for it!

The best thing would be for him to meet his friend in the morning and say to him frankly:

"We are old friends, are we not? We can speak openly. You have spoiled my happiness: there I was, the happiest man on Earth, and now I am the most miserable. I toss and turn in my bed at night, covered in sweat, and my whole body trembles. It can't go on like this. You understand me, don't you? It has to stop. Forgive me."

And would his friend then measure him up with a wordless smirk and the distracted gaze of a chicken, or a dog? Well, let him! The important thing was that his visits must end.

At about six he dressed and made himself some tea. His head felt terribly heavy, his temperature was high. Like a trained dog he knelt down next to his wife's bed and laid his tired head upon her. He wished for her to wake up, yet he did not dare rouse her. He lay there like that, quietly and calmly. On the table, the tea went cold. The sun beat its way in through a gap in the blinds. A shaft of light stole its way toward Etta's face, she awoke, and shuddered.

"What's with you, Khayim?" Her voice was filled with nervous fear.

"Nothing, Etta. I couldn't sleep so I made some tea."

"But you're trembling!"

She sat up in bed. The sight of her half-uncovered youthful body all but overpowered his senses. He fell on her with hot kisses, and forgot himself in her arms.

That night they sat outside once again—All three of them—playing cards. Khayim was tired and wanted to call it a night, but there was a curious, lively sparkle in his friend's eyes, and Etta smiled . . .

Yes, this was a new kind of beauty which he had found in her: that cold, cunning smile . . .

III

He was tormented by jealousy but what tormented him even more was the uncertainty. He did not dare speak a word of it, and he had nothing at all tangible on which to dwell. He imagined that if he ever discovered for certain that something had happened, that his

Etta had belonged to another man, then his lot would be more bearable than the current situation where he found himself being tossed from one extreme to the other, caught between love and trust in his wife on one hand, and jealousy and suspicion on the other. It would be a tragedy for him, a terrible tragedy, a black abyss would open up before him, and there would be nothing left but to cast himself inside, but at least he would no longer burn with such fever, and would no longer have to stifle the pain inside him.

"What's wrong with you Khayim? Go see a doctor." Etta would say to him.

"Oh, it's nothing . . . it comes from too much love," and he would force a smile. The phrase was intended as a kind of apology for his being somewhat cooler towards her.

Meanwhile his friend's eyes continued to sparkle; his distant gaze became intimate when he spoke to Etta. Etta smiled at her husband, and laughed aloud, whenever his friend was there.

"She never laughed like that before," he thought. "I don't like that laugh, it's too shameless. It's not like her at all."

Once, after his friend had left, he permitted himself to pass a remark:

"I've never heard you laugh like you did today."

Something akin to an angry fire flared up in her eyes, only to be extinguished a moment later. She did not respond, as though she had not heard anything.

It was only later that she sat down beside him and stroked his hair once again, smiling, once again consoling him as one consoles an angry child.

"You don't like my laugh, Khayim? You need to see a doctor about your nerves."

With that the confrontation ended, and there followed yet another tormented, sleepless night.

The next morning he asked himself again: "What grounds do I have to be so suspicious?" And once again he had to concede that he had treated his wife unfairly.

Two months passed in this way. If the first months after their wedding had counted as the happiest in his life, then these last two months were the most wretched. He felt that he lacked the patience or energy to continue suffering, that it would all be too much and, like improperly stored gunpowder, it must eventually explode. A catastrophe was surely on its way: he would lose his mind, or kill himself, or have an embarrassing outburst . . . something had to happen.

And indeed something did happen. He could not quite recall clearly how it came about. One day Etta came home complaining of a headache and went straight to bed; she fell gravely ill, and died.

On the second day of her illness she was no longer lucid and her death left many things unresolved. It all happened so quickly and incomprehensibly. Afterward old women came to sew funeral shrouds and light candles. Then her body was carried out and she was buried. He followed the funeral procession, but did not speak; he did not even cry. For some reason his friend approached him, his eyes filled with tears. Why was his friend crying? Khayim did not understand. Everything else proceeded precisely as it always does, like clockwork: illness followed by death, followed by burial, and when he got home Etta was no longer there.

The bed was empty.

He fell into a deep, heavy sleep. But in the middle of the night he awoke as if something heavy had fallen on him, and he suddenly grabbed his head and began to wail. His cries were heard only by the four walls and the empty bed beside him.

How had it come to this? When did it happen? How?

He could not even remember how many days she had been ill. It had all happened so quickly, so unexpectedly.

"This is death, death," he repeated to himself, as if only now grasping the meaning of that short word. "This is what death is!"

His friend entered, pale and dejected, his eyes bloodshot.

"Khayim! What a terrible thing! No one saw it coming . . . such a young life, such a blossoming life . . . it was all so sudden! Who could have imagined?"

And with shocked, numb eyes Khayim looked at him and answered:

"Yes, that is what death is."

They spent the night together. His friend sat down next to him on the bed and dozed off leaning against his shoulder.

Khayim shifted his weight, letting his friend's head slowly slide down onto the pillow. The physical proximity of his friend's body eased his nerves. They both slept in this position late into the night.

IV

Khayim felt compelled to hand over the running of his business to his brother, after which he left town to stay in a summer home. He was concerned about the state of his nerves, as was the doctor who examined him. He could find nothing capable of diverting or interesting him. He was unable to address anyone with more than a few curt, disjointed words—with the exception of his friend. And indeed his friend did visit him often and they spent a great deal of time together.

Mostly they spoke about Etta. He was certain that there was no other woman on earth like her. Such inner and outer harmony, such capacity for love, such a rich, tender inner life . . . When he said these things he felt his friend understood him, and this eased his pain.

"Oh, what do you know, what do you know about her beauty! The finest marble-sculpture does not possess as much beauty. With her disappearance the world has lost a work of art."

His friend listened, nodding his head, and added:

"The most beautiful woman I have ever met in my life."

Hearing these words caused something to dislodge in Khayim's heart. A shudder went through his whole body. The old jealousy was reignited in his breast.

He had held Etta in his arms—him!

Rattled by the old doubts which had suddenly been reawakened he left his friend, saying that he needed to rest.

Nights of renewed torment began for him, and the doubt gnawed at his heart like a worm. Forgotten scenes awakened in his memories. In precise detail he remembered every hand movement of Etta and his friend, every expression in their eyes, every smile; in his desire to get to the truth he weighed and measured every memory. Just as before, he lurched between faith and despair, and as before his bitterest doubts gave way to self-reproach: he was a petty, foolish man, he had no grounds for suspicion. And that most terrible of torments, uncertainty, continued to plague him. His yearning for lost happiness was pushed aside.

And as though to confirm his suspicions and heighten his unease, his friend kept his distance for several days.

When he finally saw his friend again he lost all composure and fell upon him with pleading desperation:

"You must tell me the truth; it makes no difference now anyway as she is no longer alive—tell me, was she yours? Tell the truth."

But his friend now looked at him with his absent gaze and answered as though impelled to save himself from danger:

"What are you talking about? Where would you get that idea? Nonsense! That's all in your imagination, your warped imagination."

Khayim was on the verge of tears:

"And me, vile wretch that I am, I doubted her! I was suspicious of her."

"Calm yourself, Khayim!"

Khayim tried his best to calm down, but a short while later he once again felt that he could not shake the doubts and lingering second-thoughts. He asked again:

"But tell me, what gave you the idea to speak about the beauty of her body?"

His friend exclaimed in surprise:

"What?"

"Nothing, forgive me."

And so once again he was left with his uncertainty. His instincts told him that, in order to calm himself at least a little and not be plagued day and night with the same obsession, it was better not to see his friend anymore. Let things remain as they were, in obscurity; let it remain a mystery. Let the dead be forgotten, and their secrets along with them.

Besides, he thought, there is no use in seeking happiness. Oblivion is what I need, what I need is to forget!

He moved back to the city and avoided his friend. Only then did his real mourning begin, the long suffocating longing for Etta. Her image pursued him, he felt despondent and alone in the world, alone forever. The loneliness and yearning would not leave him. There would be no third youth . . .

On mild evenings, when the anguish would not let up, and he felt the approach of a sleepless night, he would go to the cemetery, and walk by the grave of his dead wife, staring up at the night sky as it filled with stars. He thought about how fleeting it all was: the earth on which he walked, the millions of stars sparkling above, and about how everything would pass away, wither, and die, whether young, or old, whether ripe and weary, or struck down prematurely in life's full drive—these thoughts calmed and consoled him.

On one such evening, at the beginning of the month of *Khezhvn*, he met his friend—whom he had not seen in a long time—by his wife's graveside. Fresh flowers lay on her grave, which his friend had just now brought.

In that moment it became clear that his friend had hidden something from him, both during Etta's lifetime, and also now that she was dead.

"Yes, something happened between us."

He was stunned, the jealousy flowed back into his heart: he stared with wordless menace. But his friend remained calm and said:

"Tonight, it's six months to the day since her death; I brought her flowers."

"Flowers? You loved her so much?"

"Don't be angry Khayim, let's not be angry here by her graveside. This is not the place for it. Let us show respect for her and for the sanctity of our own lives."

"So that's how it is? You loved her?"

"Don't speak in that tone! Yes it's true, I loved her, and with her the best part of my life has gone, and nothing is left."

"And did she love you too?"

His friend said nothing at first, but then he approached Khayim, took him by the arm, and softly with an introspective tone said:

"Don't be angry with me, my good man; it's love. It's a force beyond our understanding, and beyond our best intentions. I loved her like no other woman on this earth."

"Oh, there isn't another like her in the world," Khayim blurted out, and he felt that with those words, the burning hatred towards his friend had vanished.

A chilly, autumnal wind blew. On the horizon the moon emerged as though bathed in blood, the trees creaked, and the wind tore off the last of their leaves.

"I have not forgotten her. She stands before me as she did in life, with her charming body, with her blonde hair and with the wonderful expression in her eyes."

But Khayim could no longer listen to his friend speak about Etta; he pulled his arm away from his friend's grasp, and walked away without saying good night.

But some months later, fortune brought the two back together. And even now—many more years have passed, and they have since grown old—they often sit together and remember Etta. With time they have grown so used to speaking about the open and hidden beauty of the dead woman that they no longer feel uncomfortable, as though they were two brothers speaking of a beloved sister who had been equally dear to them both.

1914

THEREAFTER...
(A Prose poem)

To Lipo Novogrudzki

To beauty, I came and said: "I am a person who yearns for beauty; grant me several minutes that should bring beauty to my life."

To clarity, I came and said: "I am a person who strives towards clarity; grant me several minutes to soothe my pain.

You heard my plea and gave me lies and frivolity.

... I scoured every corner of my soul, choosing the best and finest and most sublime that I possessed: each tender feeling, lucid idea and beautiful dream, every heartfelt prayer. I gathered them all together and clothed and adorned myself in them. And you emerged beautiful, intelligent, gentle and sublime, without a blemish, without a single flaw—like a god!

143

And thereafter I fell to my knees, my lips whispering a quiet prayer . . .

How divinely beautiful you were!

Now disgrace consumes my heart!

Do not come to me seeking forgiveness—it was not against me that you sinned.

In my heart lives that dark resignation: despair itself. Men flee from it—it pursues them. I have long ago stopped running; we have grown accustomed to each other, have long looked in each other's eyes and we have both laughed. It laughed at me, while I laughed at the world and at happiness.

Who can threaten me? Who can sin against me?

When an angry child strikes the marble, the marble laughs.

Do not try to console me . . .

I am the man who had the audacity to stop hoping for happiness: I am the man who had the audacity to kill every hope in his heart before it could have a chance to flower. I am the man who prefered to kill his own desires rather than have them choked by a stranger's hands.

Do you truly wish to console me?

You have blasphemed against my god . . .

Do you know the rage of a man who has run from the world, from its fear and despair, to his god; and with a bent knee and eyes filled with ecstasy, whispered a prayer—and in the midst of his devotion someone profanes his god?

That is your sin, your great transgression against my god.

And what sort of god would he be if he were capable of forgiveness? Gods that forgive crumble into pieces, like golems made of clay.

My god is a vengeful god. He cannot forgive.

Do not beg for forgiveness—you cannot beg.

You did not believe in my holiness. If you had believed. It would have been you.

Whoever lies cannot beg, and you have lied.

Your words were clichés; your tenderness was falsified; your yearning—a ruse; and your kisses were frivolity . . .

Go find your own god and beg *him* for forgiveness.

1906

AT NIGHT
(Moods and Thoughts)

The night is pitch black, one of those dark nights at month's end. Melancholy has driven me from my room and, in thrall to the darkness and the heavy silence, I meander along the tree-lined avenue in front of my house.

Midnight has been and gone. The moon has not shown its face, nor will it; last night was also moonless. The sky above my head is obscured by a heavy fog: I can discern only a few stars—each at a remove from the last—whose dim shine seems to float upward into the heavens, as though unwilling to come down to the black earth. I am surrounded on all sides by darkness and a deep heavy slumber.

My melancholy begins to leave me slowly and the space it leaves in my heart is filled with a gentle tranquility. My soul is appeased, as though I had just cried my heart out and a kind sister has wiped away my tears. A thought accompanies me on my path, that I alone am awake while the whole world around me sleeps.

All alone! Heaven and earth, darkness and shine—I take them all into myself, because I am alive.

"*Gr—gr—gr,*" a voice answers me from the stillness. Someone else is awake, just like me, among all those who sleep. Who is it? A little worm? What does it want in the dark of night? Why does it disturb the silence? I approach the curb's edge and the sound grows still. It must have heard my footsteps as I approached and fell silent in fear. For a few minutes I stand on the spot, holding my breath. And then the sound again: "*Gr—gr—gr.*" Tentatively I reach out and touch the nearby tree with my fingers: the leaves rustle and the creature falls quiet once again. The stillness around me feels so innocent and calm. But I am no longer alone: I know now for certain that in the grass next to me hides a worm, which feels my proximity just as I feel its, afraid of me because I am frightening. And who knows? Perhaps the creature is asking itself the same questions as I am: *Who is this, who disturbs the silence, my silence; who is it who interrupts the peace, my peace?* "*Gr—gr—gr,*" it calls out again, weaker and more muffled than before. Yes, it is asking. If it possesses a head its head is asking; if not, it is asking with its every limb. It asks and will never ever receive an answer. Between one creature and the next, the Creator has erected a border, an eternal frontier that no living being shall ever cross. Separate, alone, and forsaken are we creatures of the Earth, each of us groping in the dark—between one animal and another, between one person and another, between everything that has a soul, there stands a line that cannot be breached.

And if we should live a thousand years, no matter how much we speak or chirp, there is no one who will hear or understand our words or chirping. Futile is the speech, and vanity is the proliferation of words with which we seek to express our feelings in the hope that someone will hear them, that someone will understand them. He who hears, hears only his own voice; while he who understands, understands only himself. And the impressions of our souls will soon be lost along with us.

Indeed, in darkness we arrived, and in darkness we shall take our leave. The rustle of the branches, caressed by a breeze, seems to respond to my thoughts: darkness, darkness without limit, without end . . .

And the best thing man could do in life, I think to myself, would be to keep silent, to close up and nail down his heart, and hide away his pain deep inside himself, where no one should know of it, and nothing should be tainted or diminished by it . . .

And the trees suddenly become still, as though they too are reminded how vain and futile it is to express themselves, and they make peace with the realization that silence is the best course of action. ———

The darkness around me grows ever thicker. I sit down on a bench in the middle of the avenue, and my gaze penetrates deep into the obscurity. A terrible fear befalls me: I am afraid to move, afraid to budge even a hand or a foot . . . the silence and the darkness around me appear like a living being, one which is stronger than me and which dominates my will. My eyes close. I sit like this, hoping to doze off in order to weaken my terror.

I no longer see the darkness around me, but the darkness within me is all encompassing. Then I hear the howl of a dog. Its voice is terrible, truly terrible. Other dogs take up his howl in response, and a heavy, oppressive lament of heartache swirls in the air, impossible to bear. Powerlessness, and suffering without end: *O—u———u, O—u———uw*. The howl pierces my soul and my bones. I imagine that it is a horde of black hounds burying their happiness, mourning and giving eulogies: *O—u———w* lost is happiness, lost forever is their daylight. *O—u———w* and we and all our children and grandchildren shall live like this in the darkness for as long as the world lasts.

TRANSLATOR'S POSTFACE

In the nineteenth century Jewish literature was dominated by the Haskalah (Yid: *haskole*) or so-called
Jewish Enlightenment, a movement with aimed to
foster the notion of a secular Jewish education in line
with Western European ideals, and also to transform
the Hebrew language from a liturgical language into
a vehicle for contemporary scientific, philosophical
and political ideas. The readership for such works in
Hebrew was limited and so the Maskilim (proponents
of the Haskalah) turned to Yiddish, the vernacular language of the Jewish masses, in order to propagate their
ideas. This development would later, in turn, gave rise
to the Yiddishist movement, a cultural and linguistic
campaign which aimed to elevate the status of Yiddish
(which had long been disparaged as a crude "jargon",
lacking in grammar or sophistication) bringing it in line
with the modern European languages, and providing it
with a secular education and publishing infrastructure.

The watershed mark of the Yiddishist movement
was the Czernowitz Language Conference of 1908,
held in the Austro-Hungarian city of Czernowitz,

Bukovina (modern day Chernivtsi, Ukraine) which published the resolution[1] that Yiddish, alongside Hebrew, was a modern language of the Jewish people, with a burgeoning high culture.

And so by the early twentieth century, the literatures of both Hebrew and Yiddish (often the work of bilingual authors) had achieved high standards of literary quality. This period of bilingual cooperation was brief, and within a generation the ideological rivalry between Hebraists and Yiddishists (with notable exceptions) would become increasingly pronounced.

Modern Hebrew would go on to become one of the building blocks for a new Jewish national identity with Palestine as its center, while Yiddish became an international diaspora literature, seeing the development of new hubs in Western Europe, the Soviet Union, and the Americas, with an aesthetic range stretching from the deceptively folksy orality of satirist Sholem Aleichem, to the avant garde exuberance of modernist writers in the interwar period.

Yiddish Decadence

The years from the last decade of the nineteenth century until roughly the First World War, when Yiddish literature was making its decisive steps toward modernity, coincided with a time when the prevailing currents of Eastern European literature were seeped in

---

1 The wording of which was suggested by Nomberg himself.

the ambient influences—both first-hand and indirectly filtered through other artistic movements—of Western European Decadence and Symbolism.

One of the methods used by the Yiddishists to kickstart the formation of a wide-ranging literary corpus was the undertaking of large-scale translation projects. One such project, which Nomberg contributed to, was Avrom Reyzen's literary journal *Eyropeishe Literatur,* which began publishing in 1910 and ran for thirty-nine issues. The journal published new works of Yiddish literature alongside established authors from Europe and beyond, including Yiddish translations of texts by Oscar Wilde, Catulle Mendès, Paul Verlaine, Stéphane Mallarmé, Edgar Allen Poe and many others. In such a context it was inevitable that Yiddish literature would soak up influences from these authors.

In the past, scholars of Jewish literature have tended to focus on its unique aspects, studying its internal development—as though it existed in a hermetically sealed world of its own—at the expense of acknowledging the porous nature of literary influence. This tendency has resulted in a sidelining of certain authors from the literary canon, particularly in English translation.[1] With hindsight, however, it is difficult to ignore the impression that a certain cadre of Yiddish writers were working within a genre that was decidedly Decadent

---

1 Recent translations have done much to remedy this skewed image. See: Jonah Rosenfeld, *The Rivals and Other Stories*, trans. Rachel Mines, Syracuse University Press, 2020, and Mikhah Yosef Berdichevsky, *From a Distant Relation*, trans. James Adam Redfield, Syracuse University Press, 2021.

in its aesthetic sensibilities, though few of them would ever use the term directly. Where Yiddish decadence was recognized as a genre in its own right, it was categorized disparagingly as a failure of imagination:

"The truth is we have no artists with decadent souls, only ones who feign decadence in pursuit of fashion. Peretz does this, as does Hirshbeyn, even Jonah Rosenfeld. But it all rings hollow. The mimicry is all too obvious. We read it and we are left as cold as ice; all these affectations come to naught."[1]

I. L. Peretz, Hersh Dovid Nomberg, Zalman Shneour, Jonah Rosenfeld, M. Y. Berdichevsky, I. D. Berkowitz, Anna Margolin—each, at least for a time, were influenced by the prevailing Decadent atmosphere, exploring motifs such as decay, confusion, the worship of despair and the power of the irrational.

Like their Western European counterparts, Yiddish writers also experimented with fairy-tale-like stories of the fantastic and the macabre, or tales set in exotic lands. Often categorized as "folkloristic motifs", these stories bare scant relation to any real folklore tradition, let alone the Jewish one, and can only be understood in dialogue with Western European Decadence and Symbolism, as they invariably owe more to the fairy-tales of Oscar Wilde, or orientalist diversions, than to anything drawn from traditional Jewish sources.

---

1 Abraham Goldberg, "Di naye rikhtungen in der yidisher literatur" ["New Currents in Yiddish Literature"], *Shafungen un shafer*, New York, 1913.

Of particular note is the figure of the *Talush* (lit. up-rooted one) or *Fliglman* (named after the protagonist of Nomberg's eponymous short story), a Jewish take on the decadent anti-hero found in the early Yiddish worlds of Zalman Shneour and Hebrew writers such as David Fogel and Yosef Haim Brenner.[1]

The Fliglman is a young intellectual (usually a man) who has left behind the shtetl and the old traditions in order to live in the modern metropolis. They are invariably paralysed by inaction, plagued by neurosis, neurasthenia, hallucinations and inchoate drives they are unable to sate. They find themselves torn between the unprecedented pains of urban alienation and the thrill of new ideas, in a world where shadows seem to dance of their own accord, and the streets are humming with possibility and menace. The male Fliglman is ill-adapted to modern romance, and is rendered impotent in the face of modern women who are able to act with more agency, seemingly better suited to the new age. In some cases the Fliglman's general misanthropy can degrade into misogyny, as is the case with the protagonist of Zalman Shneour's *A Death*, or the murderous anti-heros, with heads dangerously full of Schopenhauer, found in the stories of M. Y. Berdichevsky. But occasionally we also find *Fliglwomen*, such as the heroines of Anna Margolin's short fiction: young women who abandon traditional ways in the pursuit of knowledge, art, and the intellectual life.

---

1 Lilach Nethanel. "David Vogel's Lost Hebrew Novel, Viennese Romance." *Prooftexts* 33, no. 3, 2013.

✳

Happiness and friendship; love and beauty; art and revolution—these and other themes are investigated in this current collection, by the sometimes caustic, sometimes lyrical pen of Yiddish writer Hersh Dovid Nomberg. The author probes these notions, cracking them open to reveal the illusory, often deceptive core within.

Nomberg was born in 1876 in the market town of Mszczonów (Yiddish: Ashminov) about thirty miles from Warsaw, which at the time was a provincial capital on the western edge of the Russian Empire. Orphaned at a young age, Nomberg was raised by his maternal grandfather in a devoutly religious milieu. He began publishing poems and short stories around 1900 in both Yiddish and Hebrew and joined the editorial boards of various newspapers and periodicals, publishing in Yiddish, Hebrew and Polish. Nomberg was instrumental in modernizing the Jewish press in the period when it began to expand throughout the Empire following a partial relaxation of censorship laws. While his own literary output was modest (he published no more than fifty stories in all), Nomberg was a fierce advocate for his fellow Jewish writers, offering mentorship, financial opportunities, and political legitimacy. He was one of the founding members of the Union of Jewish Writers and Journalists, and, from 1916–1920 he was active in the Folkspartay, a party dedicated to safeguarding secular Jewish cultural autonomy within the nascent Polish Republic.

Nomberg died at the age of fifty-one, having suffered from chronic lung problems for most of his life, but his legacy lived on in the names of Yiddish libraries, cultural associations, and publishing houses everywhere from Paris to Buenos Aires.

This selection of eighteen prose pieces aims to showcase several facets of Nomberg's writing, spanning the entirely of his short career, from "Alone" (1900) to the posthumously published "A Victim of Ingratitude" (1928), and ranging thematically from tales of urban alienation ("Sheyker and Shlimazl," "The Philosopher," "Spring Night"), fantastic and exotic tales ("A Night in a Field," "Punishment," "Happiness," "Raya Mano") to prose poems and contemplative sketches ("Summer Home," "She and I," "Waking").

I have arranged these stories not in strict chronological order, but in an order that I hope will deliver to the reader a varied and satisfying experience. The opening ("Summer Home") and the coda ("At Night") are of a piece in their contemplative nocturnal mood. Here the line between narrator and author seems to be at its thinnest, and we find him alone after the day's tumult has died away, kept company by strange noises, and the thoughts that creep in from the shadows.

Daniel Kennedy,
Tours, July 2021

A NOTE ON THE TEXTS

These stories were first published in the following periodicals:

"Af zumer-voynung" (Summer Home). *Der morgn-shtern*, 1907.
"Raya-mano" (Raya-Mano). *Di yidishe yugnt*, 1909.
"Sheker un shlimazl" (Sheker and Shlimazl). *Der veg*, 1905.
"A nakht afn feld" (Night in the Field). *Frilings-bleter*, 1910.
"In a yidish gevelb" (In a Jewish Shop). *Di tsukunft*, 1912.
"Aleyn" (Alone). *Der yud*, 1900.
"A plutslinge elter" (Sudden Old Age). *Der veg*, 1905.
"Di shtrof" (Punishment). *Der moment*, 1919.
"Dos glik" (Happiness). *Der tsvantsikster yorhundert*, 1900.
"Frilings-nakht" (Spring Night). *Folkstsaytung*, 1923.
"Men vekt" (Waking). *Varshaver tageblat*, 1916.
"Der filosof" (The Philosopher). *Haynt*, 1911.
"Zi un ikh" (She and I). *Bildung*, 1902.
"A korbn fun umdankbarkeyt" (A Victim of Ingratitude). *Forverts*, 1928.

"Motivn" (At the Ball and The Sinful world). *Der moment*, 1920.

"Fraynt" (Friendship). *Dos yidishe folk*, 1914.

"Dernokh . . ." (Thereafter). *Der veg*, 1906.

"Banakht" (At Night). Originally published in Hebrew. This version is based on Yitskhok Vayntroyb's Yiddish translation published in H. D. Nomberg, *Gezamlte verk, zibeter band*, Kultur-Lige, 1930.

GLOSSARY

Angel of Death: (Yid. *Malekh ha-moves*)
The Jewish Angel of Death is traditionally depicted as being covered with many thousands of eyes.

Barin:
Russian: Sir, master.

Fraylin:
Yiddish: Miss.

Gabbay:
A person who assists in running a synagogue.

Gemara: (Yid: *gemore*)
Part of the Talmud comprising rabbinical analysis of and commentary on the Mishnah.

Gerer rebbe:
The leader of the Ger Hasidic dynasty.

Hasidism/Hasid: (Yid. *khasidizm* or *khsides, khosid*)
A branch of orthodox Judaism originating in the 18th

century which rapidly gained popularity throughout Eastern Europe. The opponents of Hasidism were known as the misnagdim. The central characteristics of Hasidism include allegiance to a particular Rebbe, or spiritual leader, emphasis on individual prayer, and joyous worship involving singing, and dancing.

Haskalah: (Yid. *haskole*)
The Jewish enlightenment. Proponents of the Haskalah were known as Maskilim.

Maskil:
(see Haskalah)

Omar abaye:
"Thus spoke Abaye," a third century Talmudic sage. The following image is a reference to the Talmud:
"The Sages said of Yonatan ben Uzziel, the greatest of Hillel's students, that when he sat and was engaged in Torah study, the sanctity that he generated was so intense that any bird that flew over him was immediately incinerated": Sukkah 28a, *The William Davidson Tamud*.

Ozer dalim hoshiom no:
The words of a Hebrew devotional song. "Helper of the poor, please bring salvation."

Reb:
Yiddish honorific, equivalent to Mr. Used with full name, or first name only.

Rebbe:
In Hasidism, the spiritual leader of a Hasidic dynasty. A mentor/teacher/spiritual guide more generally.

Shabbes:
The Jewish Sabbath, beginning at sundown on Friday evening and ending on Saturday evening at dusk. Traditionally observant Jews are forbidden from all forms of work on Shabbes, including handling money, writing, traveling or making fire.

Shammes: (Yid. *Shames*)
The caretaker of a synagogue. Often translated as beadle or sexton.

Sheker/Shlimazl:
The names of the two characters are a play on the expression *Sheker un Shlimazl*, meaning "birds of a feather/a pair of scoundrels" (More literally: falsehood and misfortune).

Tallis: (Yid. *tales*) or Tallit, A fringed prayer-shawl. Worn during morning prayer.

Tefillin: (Yid. *tfiln*)
Tefillin, often called phylacteries, are small leather boxes containing tiny scrolls of parchment, worn during morning prayer, on the forehead and arm, secured by leather straps.